*D*amned if you do and damned if you don
Never mind that everything Sul
to him—that even the dream made sense
all came back to that. Damned if you do

He could be screwing himself as easily by holding onto her as by dumping Jennie once and for all. He couldn't get a handle on it either way.

Think very hard, Sullivan said. Well, he could do that.

He walked up the steps to the sturdy wooden porch he'd added on for them in happier days and used his key in the lock. He could remember a time when nobody on this quiet little street even bothered to lock their doors, when everyone felt safe.

He walked through the living room past the empty kitchen to his right and down the short narrow corridor to their bedroom and opened the door and there she lay.

He could almost hear her breathing—that was how peaceful she looked. How she could look so peaceful and be so bloated by now that it was impossible even to see the length of baling wire around her neck was a mystery to him.

He spoke to her. Tender endearments like in the old days.

She didn't answer. He hadn't expected her to.

She didn't listen.

He felt the rage rise again and fall.

For Dorothy

Macabre Ink is an imprint of Crossroad Press Publishing

First edition

and Other Stories

by JACK KETCHUM

CONTENTS

Returns

"I'm here."

"You're what?"

"I said I'm here."

"Aw, don't start with me. Don't get started."

Jill's lying on the stained expensive sofa with the TV on in front of her tuned to some game show, a bottle of Jim Beam on the floor and a glass in her hand. She doesn't see me but Zoey does. Zoey's curled up on the opposite side of the couch waiting for her morning feeding and the sun's been up four hours now, it's ten o'clock and she's used to her Friskies at eight.

I always had a feeling cats saw things that people didn't. Now I know.

She's looking at me with a kind of imploring interest. Eyes wide, black nose twitching. I know she expects something of me. I'm trying to give it to her.

"You're supposed to feed her for godsakes. The litter box needs changing."

"What? Who?"

"The cat. Zoey. Food. Water. The litter box. Remember?"

She fills the glass again. Jill's been doing this all night and all morning, with occasional short naps. It was bad while I was alive but since the cab cut me down four days ago on 72nd and Broadway it's gotten immeasurably worse. Maybe in her way she misses me. I only just returned last night from god knows where knowing there was something I had to do or try to do and maybe this is it. Snap her out of it.

"Jesus! Lemme the hell *alone*. You're in my goddamn head. *Get outa my goddamn head!*"

She shouts this loud enough for the neighbors to hear. The neighbors are at work. She isn't. So nobody pounds the walls. Zoey just looks at her, then back at me. I'm standing at the entrance to the kitchen. I know that's where I am but I can't see myself at all. I gesture with my hands but no hands appear in front of me. I look in the hall mirror and there's nobody there. It seems that only my seven-year-old cat can see me.

When I arrived she was in the bedroom asleep on the bed. She jumped off and trotted over with her black-and white tail raised, the white tip curled at the end. You can always tell a cat's happy by the tail-language. She was purring. She tried to nuzzle me with the side of her jaw where the scent-glands are, trying to mark me as her own, to confirm me in the way cats do, the way she's done thousands of times before but something wasn't right. She looked up at me puzzled. I leaned down to scratch her ears but of course I couldn't and that seemed to puzzle her more. She tried marking me with her haunches. No go.

"I'm sorry," I said. And I was. My chest felt full of lead.

"Come on, Jill. Get up! You need to feed her. Shower. Make a pot of coffee. Whatever it takes."

"This is fuckin' crazy," she says.

She gets up though. Looks at the clock on the mantle. Stalks off on wobbly legs toward the bathroom. And then I can hear the water running for the shower. I don't want to go in there. I don't want to watch her. I don't want to see her naked anymore and haven't for a long while. She was an actress once. Summer stock and the occasional commercial. Nothing major. But god, she was beautiful. Then we married and soon social drinking turned to solo drinking and then drinking all day long and her body slid fast into too much weight here, too little there. Pockets of self-abuse. I don't know why I stayed. I'd lost my first wife to cancer. Maybe I just couldn't bear to lose another.

Maybe I'm just loyal.

I don't know.

I hear the water turn off and a while later she walks back into the living room in her white terry robe, her hair wrapped in a pink towel. She glances at the clock. Reaches down to the table for a cigarette. Lights it and pulls on it furiously. She's still wobbly but less so. She's scowling. Zoey's watching her carefully. When she gets like this, half-drunk and half-straight, she's dangerous. I know.

"You still here?"

"Yes."

She laughs. It's not a nice laugh.

"Sure you are."

"I am."

"Bullshit. You fuckin' drove me crazy while you were alive. Fuckin' driving me crazy now you're dead."

"I'm here to help you, Jill. You and Zoey."

She looks around the room like finally she believes that maybe, maybe I really *am* here and not some voice in her head. Like she's trying to locate me, pin down the source of me. All she has to do, really, is to look at Zoey, who's staring straight at me.

But she's squinting in a way I've seen before. A way I don't like.

"Well, you don't have to worry about Zoey," she says.

I'm about to ask her what she means by that when the doorbell rings. She stubs out the cigarette, walks over to the door and opens it. There's a man in the hall I've never seen before. A small man, shy and sensitive looking, mid-thirties and balding, in a dark blue windbreaker. His posture says he's uncomfortable.

"Mrs. Hunt?"

"Un-huh. Come on in," she says. "She's right over there."

The man stoops and picks up something off the floor and I see what it is.

A cat-carrier. Plastic with a grated metal front. Just like ours. The man steps inside.

"Jill, *what are you doing?* What the hell are you *doing*, Jill?"

Her hands flutter to her ears as though she's trying to bat away a fly or a mosquito and she blinks rapidly but the man doesn't see that at all. The man is focused on my cat who remains focused on me, when she should be watching the man, when she should be seeing the cat-carrier, she knows damn well what they mean for godsakes, she's going somewhere, somewhere she won't like.

"Zoey! Go! Get out of here! *Run!*"

I clap my hands. They make no sound. But she hears the alarm in my voice and sees the expression I must be wearing and at the last instant turns toward the man just as he reaches for her, reaches down to the couch and snatches her up and shoves her head-first inside the carrier. Closes it. Engages the double-latches.

He's fast. He's efficient.

My cat is trapped inside.

The man smiles. He doesn't quite pull it off.

"That wasn't too bad," he says.

"No. You're lucky. She bites. She'll put up a hell of a fight sometimes."

"You lying bitch," I tell her.

I've moved up directly behind her by now. I'm saying this into her ear. I can *feel* her heart pumping with adrenalin and I don't know if it's me who's scaring her or what she's just done or allowed to happen that's scaring her but she's all actress now, she won't acknowledge me at all. I've never felt so angry or useless in my life.

"You sure you want to do this, ma'am?" he says. "We could put her up for adoption for a while. We don't have to euthanize her. 'Course, she's not a kitten anymore. But you never know. Some family..."

"I *told* you," my wife of six years says. *"She bites."*

And now she's calm and cold as ice.

Zoey has begun meowing. My heart's begun to break. Dying was easy compared to this.

Our eyes meet. There's a saying that the soul of a cat is seen through its eyes and I believe it. I reach inside the carrier. My hand passes *through* the carrier. I can't see my hand but she can. She moves her head up to nuzzle it. And the puzzled expression isn't there anymore. It's as though this time she can actually *feel* me, feel my hand and my touch. I wish I could feel her too. I petted her just this way when she was only a kitten, a street-waif, scared of every horn and siren. And I was all alone. She begins to purr. I find something out. Ghosts can cry.

The man leaves with my cat and I'm here with my wife.

I can't follow. Somehow I know that.

You can't begin to understand how that makes me feel. I'd give anything in the world to follow.

My wife continues to drink and for the next three hours or so I do nothing but scream at her, tear at her. Oh, she can hear me, all right.

I'm putting her through every torment I can muster, reminding her of every evil she's ever done to me or anybody, reminding her over and over of what she's done *today* and I think, *so this is my purpose, this is why I'm back, the reason I'm here is to get this bitch to end herself, end her miserable fucking life* and I think of my cat and how Jill never really cared for her, cared for her wine-stained furniture more than my cat and I urge her toward the scissors, I urge her toward the window and the seven-story drop, toward the knives in the kitchen and she's crying, she's screaming, too bad the neighbors are all at work, they'd at least have her arrested. And she's hardly able to walk or even stand and I think, *heart attack maybe, maybe stroke* and I stalk my wife and urge her to die, *die* until it's almost one o'clock and something begins to happen.

She's calmer.

Like she's not hearing me as clearly.

I'm losing something.

Some power drifting slowly away like a battery running down.

I begin to panic. I don't understand. *I'm not done yet.*

Then I feel it. I feel it reach out to me from blocks and blocks away far across the city. I feel the breathing slow. I feel the heart stopping. I feel the quiet end of her. I feel it more clearly than I felt my own end.

I feel it grab my own heart and *squeeze.*

I look at my wife, pacing, drinking. And I realize something and suddenly it's not so bad anymore. It still hurts, but in a different way.

I haven't come back to torment Jill. Not to tear her apart or to shame her for what she's done. She's tearing herself apart. She doesn't need me for that. She'd have done this terrible thing anyway, with or without my being here. She'd planned it. It was in motion. My being here didn't stop her. My being here afterwards didn't change things. Zoey was mine. And given who and what Jill was what she'd done was inevitable.

And I think, *to hell with Jill. Jill doesn't matter a bit.*

Not one bit. Jill is zero.

It was Zoey I was here for. Zoey all along. That awful moment.

I was here for my cat.

That last touch of comfort inside the cage. The nuzzle and purr. Reminding us both of all those nights she'd comforted me and I her. The fragile brush of souls.

That was what it was about.

That was what we needed.

The last and the best of me's gone now.

And I begin to fade.

Author's Note: Like some of my poetry and a story now and then "Returns" was an exorcism. I wrote it just for me. I'd recently had to put down my cat and felt every bit as angry, helpless and heartsick as my ghostly narrator does here.

But the story, of course, is ultimately about connection. Not loss. In that sense, it's a celebration.

—JK

Damned If You Do

"I just don't know where to go with this anymore," Brewer said.

The clock on the wall above and behind his newest patient told Sullivan that they were just under forty minutes into their fifty-minute hour.

Sullivan watched the folded arms and the tightly crossed legs come apart all at once like a man trying to unravel whatever knot lay inside him, saw the head droop slightly. He had noted this body language before with Brewer and knew it to be a sham—a dumb-show of submission to the fates—and knew it was only temporary. Brewer was tougher than that.

"I don't know what to do with her."

He shook his head. Clasped his hands. The pause lengthened.

"Are you waiting for me to tell you, John?"

"Yes. No. Oh hell, I don't know. I don't know what I'm waiting for."

"You realize that's not my job."

"Of course I do."

"My job is to help you draw your own conclusions. Make your own decisions."

"I know that. But I've come to this total impasse. Jennie just doesn't listen anymore. It's as though I'm not there. Not even in the room."

"Why do you think that's happened?"

The arms and legs snapped into place again. Privates hidden. Chest hidden. His maleness trapped once again from the outside in. He sat back rigid in his chair.

"Why now?"

"Maybe it's the work."

"The work?"

"Maybe she doesn't respect my work anymore."

That was an evasion.

"Why would that be? You're a carpenter. You make furniture. And from what you've told me about your prices you must be pretty good at it."

"Yeah, but I'm not selling the way I did. It's this damn economy. This is a tourist town for godsake. Leaf-season wasn't half what it ought to be."

"You're not poor, John. You can afford me."

That drew a smile.

"No, I'm not poor. She gets everything she needs. So maybe it's not the work or the money. I dunno. But I'm an old-fashioned guy, doc. My word used to be law around that house. The way I was brought up that's how it's supposed to be. But now..."

He sighed.

"Have you talked about it?"

"No."

"Why not?"

"I told you. I've tried. She doesn't listen!"

Sullivan watched his eyes scan the room—the simple office furniture, the painted landscapes, the open window behind his desk—as though they'd taken on a sudden interest. When in fact he'd been seeing them once a week for over two months now.

"So you feel you've got to do something, that some action on your part might change things. Is that it?"

"I've got to do *something*. End it maybe, just get her the hell out of my life. When I really don't *want* her out of my life. At least part of me doesn't. I feel like, you know, damned if you do and damned if you don't. Know what I mean?"

"You ever consider the problem might be hers to solve? Not your own?"

"Huh?'

"That maybe it's simply something *she's* going through. That maybe she should be in therapy too. It's possible."

He laughed. "She'll never be in therapy, believe me."

"Why's that?"

"She just won't."

He heard that familiar *brick wall* tone of voice of his.

Knew it was prudent to back away. *Leave it be for now,* he thought. *Try another tack.*

"You have any dreams for me today, John?"

Sullivan was a firm believer in dreams as metaphors for problems left untended-to, each with its own symbolic language. Anything from a reminder to pay that overdue gas bill to resolving the guilt over a loved-one's death. That by penetrating the meaning of these metaphors the truth of what was foremost in the mind clarified, its emotional resonance understood for what it was. A dream was a nudge in the ribs reminding you what still needed doing.

Brewer smiled. "You and your dreams. Yeah, as a matter of fact I do. Night before last. I wrote it down, like you said."

He took a folded yellow post-a-note out of his pocket. "I'm just a kid, nine or ten maybe. I'm with a younger boy, probably six or seven I guess and we're out in my yard and I have an axe. So I start hacking away with this axe at a tree-stump on the lawn while this other kid stands back watching, and the stump becomes my dog Tiger's head."

He looked up. "I really had this dog Tiger, this brown-and-white mutt, when I was about that age. Weird, huh?"

"Do you hit the dog with the axe?"

"Once. Like he turns from stump into dog mid-stroke. Like by then I'm committed to the downswing, you know? And this single drop of blood trickles down off his head and off his eye."

"That's all? One drop?"

"Yeah, like a tear. But the thing is, he *bears* it. He doesn't die or anything or run away howling like a normal dog would. He just sits there looking at me. The axe is still in his head. And then I wake up."

Sullivan wished now he'd gotten round to asking him about dreams earlier. They were nearly out of time. They'd need to go into it further next session. But he'd ask the three basic questions, anyway. He had the time for that.

"What was your day like, day before yesterday?"

He shrugged. "Nothing out of the ordinary. I was building the cabinet for the Sebald woman most of the day, took a break for lunch over at Duras' Deli, went back to work, knocked off about four-thirty, five."

"Was it going well?"

"It's a standard model. I could build it with my eyes closed by now."

"How are you at chopping wood?"

"Same thing."

"How did you *feel* in the dream? Do you recall?"

"Well, at first I guess I was having fun. Kind of showing off for this other kid, know what I mean? Then with Tiger...I'm not sure. Scared? Shocked?"

"Anything else? Like *guilt* for instance?"

"No. Not that I can remember."

"Okay. What does Tiger represent for you?'

"A dog. A dog I had as a kid."

"And what does a dog represent?

"I dunno. You trust a dog. He looks up to you. He goes where you go."

"Unconditional love?"

"That too I guess. Yeah."

"Sound like anybody you know? Or *thought* you knew?"

He grinned. "Jesus. Yeah. Sounds a little like Jennie, doesn't it."

He let that sink in for a moment.

"And I hit her in the head with an axe."

"That's right."

He had time for one last line of questioning.

"What did you say Tiger did when you hit him?"

"Nothing. He didn't do anything. Just looked at me."

"Did you get any kind of feeling from him? Read anything in his expression, maybe?"

"Nothing. Just a dog thing, you know? Those big sad eyes looking at you. Still sort of expectant I guess is the word. Like what's next? Like whatever you do, it's okay by me."

He's looking for forgiveness, Sullivan thought.

The dog will forgive him anything.

Jennie will forgive him anything.

Only not anymore.

They'd get deeper into this next time.

He stood up from behind the desk.

"I don't normally give advice, John. You're aware of that. But this once I'm going to break my rule and ask you not to do anything over the coming week you might regret later. I'm not talking about inaction. You go ahead and do what you have to do. Only think about it very hard beforehand. Okay?"

"Okay."

And after the man left Sullivan wondered why he'd said that. It wasn't like him. A patient learned by his mistakes as much as by anything else. But despite his disclaimer about going ahead and doing what you have to do he'd essentially told Brewer to hang in there for a week and wondered why.

He thought it possibly had to do with the single part of the dream they hadn't touched upon yet—the watchful boy in the background. Somehow the boy disquieted him.

His next patient was due in five minutes. He'd think it over this evening. Maybe talk to the wife.

Ella was a good listener.

Damned if you do and damned if you don't.

Never mind that everything Sullivan had said made sense to him—that even the dream made sense to him now to a degree—it all came back to that. Damned if you do and damned if you don't. He could be screwing himself as easily by holding onto her as by dumping Jennie once and for all. He couldn't get a handle on it either way.

Think very hard, Sullivan said. Well, he could do that.

He walked up the steps to the sturdy wooden porch he'd added on for them in happier days and used his key in the lock. He could remember a time when nobody on this quiet little street even bothered to lock their doors, when everyone felt safe.

He walked through the living room past the empty kitchen to his right and down the short narrow corridor to their bedroom and opened the door and there she lay.

He could almost hear her breathing—that was how peaceful she looked. How she could look so peaceful and be so bloated by now that it was impossible even to see the length of baling wire around her neck was a mystery to him.

He spoke to her. Tender endearments like in the old days.

She didn't answer. He hadn't expected her to.

She didn't listen.

He felt the rage rise again and fall.

He took a moment to admire the craftsmanship of the knotty pine box he had made for her which exactly fit the length of the bed from headboard to baseboard and thought suddenly for a moment of the boy—the younger boy watching in his dream. He realized that he had never seen or could not remember the face of the boy. He doubted it mattered.

Dump her? Or leave her be? he thought.

It was possible he could wait until his next session with Sullivan but he didn't know. He wasn't sure.

She was really beginning to stink.

Somewhere around the time I was writing *She Wakes* and *The Girl Next Door* I was in therapy for a couple of years. Eventually I worked out what was troubling me. But I was very aware that you keep some secrets even from your therapist.

Consider Tony Soprano.

The dream about the dog Tiger occurred to me one night many years later. I decided it was perfect for my little hide-and-go-seek therapy session.

—JK

Station Two

*Shortly before the incident in the restaurant Santorini
this was how things stood.*

"Talk to me, Hal," Jan Resnick was saying. "Why won't you please just talk to me?"

Hal Reese sat looking out the window into the bright New York City night and pedestrians passing, headlights passing, delivery boys on old beat-up bikes pedaling against traffic, his body at an angle only slightly facing her. His legs were crossed and his left foot tapped impatiently into space. *The left foot wanted to go somewhere. The right was rooted to the floor.* There was food on the table, lemon chicken for him and stuffed grape leaves for her. *Roasted bird and fallen leaves.*

As yet they hadn't touched it.

He drank his scotch. By now her coffee would be tepid. She hadn't touched that either. Jan watched his head turn to track a pretty brunette in a white tee-shirt, tights and headphones. Ordinarily she wouldn't have minded his watching the brunette. Now suddenly everything he did seemed to frighten her.

"*Three years,* Hal."

"In December. It's only August."

"I put you through school for godsakes."

"You made the cash, sure. I put myself through school."

Even through the fear and sadness it galled her.

"All our expenses. The rent. *Everything.* On my feet all day, just like this poor kid you just snapped at over the goddamn fish."

"I told you. You'll get half the back rent and half the bills. I've already figured it. You want the amount? The fish was overdone."

He sounded bored to death with the whole thing.

Bored with her.

Just like that.

The announcement had come out of the blue right there in the restaurant not half an hour ago. They'd ordered and then he told her. He'd be packing over the weekend. He'd be leaving Sunday morning. He was sorry.

He didn't sound sorry.

They'd fucked just the night before. Jesus!

He was leaving her for another woman, of course. Hal would always have to have a woman. Somebody to take care of him, mother him, flatter him, fuck him. He couldn't stand to be alone. Jan even knew who she was. Liddy Krest, trader for another firm, she couldn't remember which. They'd met a few times at parties. Jan had found her cold and somewhat abrasive but forgave that right away. It would not be an easy thing to be a woman on the floor of the Stock Exchange. It was pretty much a man's world and the competition brutal.

Her eyes blurred over. She'd started to cry again. She reached across the table. Touched the back of his hand.

"Hal, look at me. Look at me."

She wanted him to see the pain, to *gaze* into the pain.

To see what he was doing.

He wouldn't.

"Hal. Please. Don't do this."

The restaurant was busy. She wondered if anyone heard the desperation in her voice. Heard and found her pitiful. She was begging. She wondered if passers-by could see it on her face through the plate-glass windows that boxed their corner table. Had she known this was coming she might at least have picked a place less exposed to strangers.

Hal might have picked one for her.

He hadn't. He didn't care.

How could that be?

She'd thought he'd always care.

They'd talked marriage. Children.

He stared out the window at all the passing faces.

Jan Reznick allowed herself the tears.

Diane Farrell wasn't having the best of nights behind the bar.

Though she'd sure as hell had a whole lot worse.

A few years back she'd worked for this mob-connected joint down in Little Italy. Walked into the office one night to get change for the register and found the owner in his swivel chair behind the desk getting a blowjob from a waitress. Her boss made change from the cashbox. The waitress never missed a beat.

The same night some asshole puked into his beer.

It was that kind of place.

Then another night they're packed, roaring, and she's on with this girl Susan, absolutely useless as a bartender but pretty enough to draw the wiseguys like hounds on a rabbit and Diane's down at the end of the bar mixing drinks for the tables when suddenly Susan starts screaming. She turns and sees eight of *the boys* as her boss calls them—gold chains, open shirts and hairy chests, Atlantic City blondes on their arms, the whole bit—out of their chairs and beating hell out of this little Mexican delivery boy, just a kid. Chairs are flying. Tables falling. Women screaming.

Somebody calls the cops. And the cops arrive so quickly you had to figure they were just *waiting* for something to happen in this joint. One of *the boys* ducks behind the bar, hands her a pistol, says *hi I'm Tommy* or whatever and tells her that if she's asked, she's to say he's worked here for months, just another bartender. She's shaking so bad she can barely get the pistol hidden down into the ice. The cops question her and she says she saw absolutely nothing, she was busy, she missed the whole thing but they don't believe her, they take her ID and threaten her with arrest for withholding evidence until finally she's so damn scared she's sobbing. At which point the cops back off, take a few more names and leave.

Tommy or whatever his name is pulls his gun out of the ice and kisses her. Shoves his tongue down her throat. His breath is worse than Godzilla's.

Thanks, babe.

About a gallon of Absolut later she finally gets rid of the taste of him.

She'd had worse nights, oh yeah. But this one was bad enough.

First of all nobody in the whole damn place was tipping. You'd think it was the day after Christmas or something, when nobody's got a spare cent to their name. This, just two nights after she's moved into a new apartment, with a month's rent up front, a month's rent security and a month's rent to the agent. Not to mention Con Ed, Manhattan Cable, Bell Atlantic and the movers. Then around seven thirty some business type has four tequila sunrises and while she's down at the espresso machine he waltzes out the door. So she's twenty dollars out-of-pocket on this joker.

She's practically working for free here.

Then there was just the mood of the place. On any given night it's usually the manager who creates the mood among the employees and that was definitely the way it was here tonight. Theodoro had walked in a few minutes late at about quarter after five with what appeared to be a hard-on for whoever he laid eyes on. Busboys, waiters, everybody. With Theo it happened sometimes. Nothing was right. The linen wasn't folded correctly. Place-settings were crooked. There were spots on a tablecloth. Tonight Lindsey had forgotten to fill a bowl of sugar packets on a table at section three. You'd think she'd stood up on it and started dancing on the thing.

And all *Phil* did was to talk to her across the bar for a couple of minutes about the Yankee game. Theo had reamed him a whole new asshole for that one.

"Get your section down! Stop hanging around! Stop the bullshitting! You get paid to do a job, do it!"

God!

A couple of minutes. Where's the harm?

Even one of the cooks got a piece of him about an hour ago. Usually the cooks were exempt from that. You didn't want them to screw up the food sort of accidentally-on-purpose. But that didn't stop him tonight.

Theo was on the rag *bigtime.*

She felt bad for all of them and especially for Phil. Like it was partly her fault for encouraging him. It was true Phil seemed to have a thing for her and wanted to talk at every opportunity. He was a shameless flirt but he was harmless and it was still early for godsakes. They hadn't been busy at all at the time. Plus Phil's section that night was section two. Only eight doubles, sixteen place-settings total and only one table then in use. A pair of old ladies sipping martinis. He wasn't the greatest waiter in the world but he wasn't the worst either. He could handle a couple of old ladies.

But Theo's barking at him had unnerved him.

Around eight-thirty word got to her through Lindsey—who everybody knew was dating the guy—that Phil had spilled oil on a customer. A woman's pink leather jacket no less. Which meant he'd have to pick up the tab for her dry-cleaning. A *pink leather jacket?* Who in the hell wears pink leather anyway?

Around nine he dropped a plateful of *moussaka*.

Luckily there was nobody under it.

Everybody heard it shatter.

You could see that Theo was livid. But by then the restaurant was busy. He wouldn't have time to get on Phil's case for a while.

He had to smile nice for the customers.

But Phil wasn't going to be doing any more flirting with her tonight, that was for sure. It was too bad, really. Phil was from Tennessee and his accent was sweet. She thought he was cute in a soft, boyish way. And Diane wasn't any kid anymore. She didn't mind him flirting with her at all. As for Lindsey, she didn't seem to care one way or the other. She guessed they weren't that serious.

She poured a draft of Amstel Lite for one of the suspendered-and-power-tied yuppies toward the front of the bar who would probably not tip her either and thought how it would be nice to go home to her boyfriend Steve and have an Absolut and lie down with him and make love on their brand new mattress and maybe unpack a box or two or maybe not.

Instead the night droned on.

It was hard to look at the woman facing him over John's shoulder and just as hard not to. It made him think of what *he* must have looked like that final night with Greg. He guessed that gay or straight, heartbreak was heartbreak.

It was written all over her.

He watched her reach across the table and had to look away.

"There were a whole bunch of us back then," John was saying, "most of us living within about ten blocks of each other up here. James and I'd been lovers back in high school, we went back *that* far. But then there was his new lover and my new lover and his *old* lover and all these people we'd met. A lot of them theatre people because of James—actors, costume-makers, directors. Louis played trumpet for some Broadway shows. Alan was an off-off-Broadway playwright. But there were also a lot like me in the health-care business. Speech therapy, P.T. And we used to complain about how awful conditions were in these various facilities we were working in."

"I know," Danny said. "Before my mom died, for a while there I was shopping around for a place for her. With the osteoporosis she couldn't live alone and we didn't think we could afford a full-time nurse at the time. Everything I looked at was so *fucking* depressing."

He was swearing too much. He made a mental note to watch it. He'd only slept with John once and dated him twice before that. But it was enough to know that John Walters hardly ever swore. And probably didn't care for it much. John was a little old-fashioned. He liked that.

You're already half-hooked on the guy, he thought. *Watch your mouth.*

John nodded, adjusted his Calvin Klein glasses and sipped his Heineken. "Yes, but your mom was out in New Jersey. You think the places *you* saw were bad, you should see some of the ones in the City. Anyway a bunch of us were talking one night. Back then it didn't look like any of us were ever going to make any real money to speak of—this was way before the boom in healthcare—so what we decided was, when retirement-time came around, we'd pool whatever cash we did have and buy this big old house somewhere out in the boonies and by then the various health-care people would have made all these connections so we'd staff the place ourselves. Take care of ourselves. A communal thing. We'd call it Queen's End."

The waiter was a sandy-haired kid with bright blue eyes and beautiful skin who didn't look old enough to be serving drinks. He saw them laughing and smiled.

"Can I get you folks another round?" he said.

"Sure," said John. "Same thing?"

"Same thing. Dewars rocks for me and a Heineken. Thanks."

The waiter moved away.

"Queen's End. That's a hoot. You still going to do it?"

John sighed. "So many people have moved away, you know? We've lost touch. It's kind of sad, really. We were a pretty neat bunch

I think. Smart, talented. Who knows? We might have even made it happen."

They laughed again. One of the things Danny Martino liked about John was his laugh. It had an honest sound. The way his father used to laugh before the cancer. Before his mother's bones became brittle as glass.

Beyond him the woman put her hands up over her eyes. Her shoulders were shaking.

"God, I hate to see that."

"See what?"

"The woman behind you. I think her boyfriend or her husband or something just dumped her. I noticed her a while ago. She's crying."

"What's he doing? The boyfriend."

"Just sitting there. Unless I read the body-language all wrong he really couldn't give a shit."

There he was, swearing again. He shook his head.

"Men, huh?"

"Yeah. Men."

"You should do it."

"Do what?"

"Queen's End."

John smiled.

They could never know what it was like.

And Theo wasn't about to tell them.

At home on his island of Thera he'd waited tables himself. If they thought the work was hard here they should try it at an outdoor *taverna* on the slope of a mountain. In summer the tourists were like a biblical plague of locusts, a blight on the land—the Americans impatient, the Germans imperious, the Australians drunk and sloppy. Tips were poor, the British in particular were cheap bastards. You bussed your own tables. You were overworked and understaffed and the hours stretched on forever.

He was grateful to his cousin Tasos for bringing him to this country and giving him first a waiter's job and now this one—he had two sisters and an aging mother he would like to bring over himself one day. He was saving for that. No drinking, no carousing.

His bank account grew steadily. But the work came at some personal price too. In his painstakingly written letters to his cousin he'd lied about the extent of his command of the English language. That was one thing.

By island standards it was good. Here it was just passable. He'd become aware of that right away. So had his cousin.

To his credit Tasos refrained from shipping him back on the next available flight. Theo promised to study and he *did* study and his ears were always open for some new word or phrase. His problem, of course, was with the American vernacular. Words were often absent from his Greek-English dictionary when he went to look for them and he was not about to reveal to anyone for whom English was their first language that he did not know the meaning of *shitcanned* or *wasted* or *don't get your balls in an uproar.*

Tasos and he agreed that dignity was important. *Santorini* was a dignified restaurant and would stay that way. As would its management. So he suffered his deficiencies in silence and continued to read and study.

He knew that in general he wasn't liked here. There was something stiff in his manner. Part of it was his language problem, he knew. In some infuriating way he felt inferior to his staff, to these Americans in their twenties, just children really—he, Theodoro Vassiliades, a grown man of thirty-two. It was humiliating.

He knew he was often short with them. He knew he had a temper. Like tonight. The subway had been late again and usually he reckoned that possibility into his travel-time but this time he'd neglected to do so. So yes, he was short with them though he knew he shouldn't be, that this was counterproductive. But they were born with all the advantages of knowing nearly from birth the most powerful language in the world. He doubted that one of them knew a word of Greek that was not on the menu and even those they managed to mispronounce frequently. Theo was quick to correct them.

But another part of it was simply his own nature. He had always been reserved, even on Thira, even as a boy. In that he was like his father. He had not had a woman, for instance, until he was twenty-five. And then the experience was so disheartening he did not even try to have another until over a year later.

His reserve had always made him lonely.

Here there was no one. He'd tried with American women, god knows. But something about him always seemed to put them off. After one date, maybe two, they'd lose interest. Perhaps when he *did* talk he talked too much about his homeland, his island, about growing up there and the sunny days and the nights full of stars. Perhaps they thought him hopelessly unsophisticated, hopelessly sentimental. Thus, in the American vernacular, a *loser*. He'd noted that men here had an insouciance and an edge to them, some fundamental ease and toughness of manner both of which angered him because they were postures he could not begin to muster. So did many of the women. Not all but some.

This one, now. Lindsey.

He'd yelled at her earlier over the sugar packets. He shouldn't have.

Scolding was not the way to charm an American woman, even one as young as Lindsey. She'd been glowering at him ever since.

Her pale brow would knot, the pretty blue eyes would flash.

It made him both sad and angry.

He watched her hand out menus to a table of three he'd just seated, two young men and a woman. They were smiling. *She* was smiling. Then she said something which made them laugh. She laughed too.

He had not made anyone laugh for a long time now.

The door opened and a couple stepped in. He guessed them to be in their forties. Well dressed, attractive. The man had all the poise and grace of a successful American male and Theo simply couldn't help it—he resented the man on sight.

"Good evening, sir. Good evening, madam."

"Could we have one over by the window?"

"Certainly, sir. Right this way."

He led them to station two and smiling, pulled out the chair for the lady.

The sandy-haired young waiter's smile did silent battle with his frown as he handed them the menus. *Guess he's having a rough night,* she thought.

Evelyn Wolper opened hers and glanced it over. *Dolmades. Spanakopita. Taramasalata. Moussaka. Calamares.* The waiter asked them about drinks and Kenneth asked for their best red Greek wine. *Right away, sir,* said the waiter and moved away.

Kenneth picked up his own menu.

"Okay," he said. "Previews of coming attractions.

Where do we start?"

She smiled. "God, I am *so* glad we're doing this. You won't be sorry. You're going to love it there."

"I believe you. But what do we *order*?"

"I'll go easy on you. Start with the mixed warm meses.We'll split them. You're going to love the *kefthedes*, I think. Then if I were you I'd go for the chicken *lemono* or the *souvlakia*."

"Souvlaki I've had."

"Then try the chicken. It's roasted on a horizontal grill and basted with lemon, oil and herbs. Mostly mint and oregano. It's delicious."

"What about you?"

"I haven't had *moussaka* in ages. It's good here. I'll give you a taste. That and a small Greek salad, I guess."

"Feta?"

"Feta. I can't believe I've finally gotten you to try Greek food."

He shrugged. "Meat and potatoes man."

"The chicken comes with potatoes."

"I noticed that."

They put down their menus and she reached over for his hand. He gave hers a squeeze and smiled.

"Two and a half weeks. In my favorite place in the world. I can't believe it. No phones, no clients. Thank you, Kenneth."

"You're quite welcome, Mrs. Wolper."

"It is a second honeymoon, isn't it?"

"Yes it is. And you know what? Now that I've gotten used to the idea, I might just be as happy about this trip as you are." He shook his head. "How about that?"

"How about that."

The waiter arrived and poured the wine. Kenneth swirled, tasted and pronounced it fine. He filled their glasses. They didn't even bother letting go of each other's hands while he was pouring. It felt almost as though they were kids again. She remembered that the waiter had been frowning and smiling, both, when he greeted them. She glanced up and read no expression on his face at all now.

He simply poured the wine.

A young couple got up next to them and moved away. She saw the waiter glance at the table, at the tip on the table, and watched the frown reappear again.

They placed their order. The waiter said *thank you*, scooped up his tip and turned toward the kitchen.

"Athens is a bore," she said. "One night in the Plaka and then we're out of there. Mykonos first, and then either Thira or Criti."

"Criti?"

"Crete."

"I've got to read up on this."

"Yes, you do. Be a change from all those briefs, won't it."

He sipped the wine. "Yes it will. Damn," he said. "This really *is* a decent wine."

She smiled again, a secret smile. This was right. This was going to be the perfect spark to a slightly tired but still affectionate marriage. She'd *known* it.

Back home in Athens, Tennessee, Philip Auton had not been one known for anger. Quite the opposite. The good-looking, intelligent son of a successful pharmacist and a respected registered nurse he'd always had it easy—so it was easy to be easygoing. With family, with friends and especially with women. In high-school plays he always got the lead and more often than not the leading lady. Same thing in State College.

His more *private* private life was his own business and thus far still that way.

New York was a whole other thing.

New York was a series of brick walls.

He got good parts in bad showcases that nobody came to see unless you counted the asshole families of playwright, director, cast and crew. More a circle-jerk than professional theatre. He got callbacks for commercials. One for a soap.

He got a job as a waiter. A fucking *waiter*.

Oh, you're an actor? So what restaurant you work at?

The old joke wasn't funny. Not one bit.

He got lucky on a sublet from an acting buddy down on the

Lower East Side. But even that was going down the tubes by the end of summer. His buddy was returning from stock in Massachusetts. So Phil was already searching around in every spare moment for something he could somehow *possibly* afford. What he'd seen was sure not encouraging. Probably he'd wind up in some hole down on Avenue A, the ass-end of nowhere, at the rate he was going. Or worse, he'd have to go back to his smug little town with his tail between his legs and get a job with his father.

He'd thought maybe Lindsey would help, that maybe they could move in together. Her place was just a few blocks north of the restaurant. He could walk to work. Would have made at least that part of his life nice and cozy. He'd broached the subject just the night before over beers at the World Café.

No way, she said. *Fucking's one thing. But living together? I've seen your apartment, Phil. No offense but you're a slob. Unh-unh. Not in a billion years.*

He didn't know what the hell to say to that shit so he paid the tab and walked on her.

Then all day today she'd frosted him.

Like he'd offended her by even asking.

Bitch.

Between her frosting him and Theo mouthing off to him earlier—fucking him up *especially royally* since he'd been working up to asking Diane, who'd moved just a couple days ago, if maybe *she* could use a roommate—he was already *major* pissed off by the time he spilled the olive oil on the blonde bitch's pink leather jacket. Even more pissed off dropping the *moussaka*. Seeing it there splattered all over the floor in front of him his brain started buzzing like a tuning fork, he had to will his heart to stop racing.

It looked like something he'd seen as a kid in the woods in good old fucking Athens, Tennessee.

All in all he was having one hell of a night. Theo kept watching him like he was afraid he'd steal the cutlery. It was weird because he was an actor and should have been used to people watching him but this was different.

It was like Theo was *willing* him to screw up again.

Well dammit, he wasn't going to. He didn't want this cracker-ass job but god knows he needed it. He hated needing it but he did and that was that.

Lindsay and Theo, they could both go fuck themselves.

The greasy little Greek prick wasn't even an American.

Smile, he thought. *Work the room. You know how.*

You always do.

He was thinking all this and washing his hands in the men's room after taking his leak and zipping his fly, gazing at himself in the mirror and smiling and judging he looked fine, just fine, that nobody would know how pissed he was, nobody would guess a thing. The tips were going to *fly*. When he walked out into the restaurant again the old bag lady was just coming in off the sidewalk, headed toward his station.

From the bar Diane saw her sit at table five just beyond the pair of men who were far too good-looking to be anything but gay and adjust the pair of overstuffed dirty shopping bags at her feet. Theo was seating a party of six at station four, pulling together a pair of tables so that his back was to the woman. Theo hadn't noticed.

Lindsay had and she was wondering if Phil might be needing some backup. She was breaking up with him, sure, any day now, there was something too childish and self-centered about the guy, even more than you'd expect from an actor but they worked together and that was no reason to leave him high and dry with the problem of the old lady. She hesitated, watching the two men and an oriental couple two tables away register first the stink of her and then the actual presence behind them. The middle-aged couple directly beside her put down their glasses of red wine and were trying not to stare. Lindsay worked her way through the tables and got to Phil's side just as he was asking her, red-faced but politely, if she had any money to pay for whatever it was she'd ordered. With that the woman stood up and began to scream. She instinctively backed away.

"You think I got no money? Fucking *sonovabitch*! You ask *them* if they got any money? You ask *them*?" She swept the room with her arm.

"*Fucking cocksucker per-jidice shit-eatin' motherfuck whore-fucker!* You ask *them*?"

By then Theo was moving fast across the room and other than Phil murmuring something, trying to calm her, and the woman's hoarse screaming you could've heard a pin drop, every eye in the place was on them as Theo stepped up behind him and Phil reached out to take her by the arm and that was when she shoved him. He wasn't expecting that and neither was Theo and they both fell back into table six, hit it hard and slid to the floor. The bottle of red wine the couple was drinking flew off the table and exploded like a bomb at the two gay men's feet. The woman's half-full glass jumped into her lap. The man's glass was in his hand and he must have involuntarily grasped it harder because the stem snapped and suddenly the man was bleeding.

Diane grabbed a clean linen napkin, ducked under the counter and hurried over.

By then Theo'd recovered. He was up on his feet and hustling the woman, still screaming *cocksucker motherfucker* but offering little resistance now, out the door. Phil got up and stood there looking stunned. Lindsay was attending to the woman, dabbling at the wine-stain on her skirt, unaware that the man was bleeding. In fact Diane got to him just as the *wife* noticed.

"Oh my god," she said.

"Here, let me wrap this around it. Let's get you into the men's room." The wound was between thumb and forefinger and looked deep. She wrapped the linen tight and got him to his feet. The man was turning white. His wife got up and followed them. Diane turned to Lindsay.

"There's a first-aid kit in the desk upstairs in the office. Get it."

Lindsay nodded.

One of the two gay men was using a water-soaked napkin on the cuff of his once cream-colored pants-leg when Theo returned for the bag-lady's filthy shopping bags. The man was smiling in a good-natured way and shaking his head as though to say, *hey, it's New York City, right?* Theo saw Phil doing nothing, just standing there. He hefted the foul-smelling bags and shot him a look.

"Goddammit, Phil. Help the man. Get him some seltzer. Get a mop for godsakes or call a busboy or something. For god's sake *do* something!"

What Phil *did* actually do surprised everybody.

There were two glass coffeepots, regular and decaf, both almost full, on burners at the waiter's station.

Phil's ears were ringing. He could feel the blood pounding in his head. Somebody had knocked him down. Somebody had shouted at him. Somebody had frosted him. Somebody was bleeding.

He wanted to cry. He wanted to scream.

He picked up the pots of coffee and walked back to station two. The faggot was still bending over dabbing at his pants leg but he got the other one, the one without the glasses as he swung the decaf in a wide arc yelling *refill, folks?* in his best and loudest stage voice, splashed the other faggot in the face so that he screeched and fell into the puddle of wine on the floor but the one he *really* got was the arrogant-looking prick who'd complained about the fish, him and his mousy girlfriend, got them so bad they both fell back off their chairs, the guy falling *through* the plate-glass window out to the sidewalk and he watched with fascination as a slab of glass as big as the table they'd been sitting at slid free of its metal sash like a see-through guillotine and damn near separated the cocksucker's head from his body.

People in the other sections were screaming right along with him, some weird choral music and mobbing the doorway so that Theo had to push his way through, Theo looking scared and furious but coming at him all the same the stupid fuck and he could hear the cooks yelling in Greek and Spanish and heading for the back door as he whirled and smashed the pot of regular against the left side of Theo's head but then didn't even wait to see him slide and fall. He leaned over the service-counter to the kitchen and it was as though the cooks had left the cleaver sitting there just for him just for his own personal use, his personal favorite weapon of choice so he headed toward the men's room, Lindsay the first one curious about all the commotion outside so that her head was the first he used it on *bye bitch* and then he had to tug the damn thing free of her which was not the way it was with the doggies and kitties back in Tennessee, more difficult than that and by the time he got it out of her fallen body they were on him, all of them, the bleeding guy and his wife and even Diane for god's sake *even her* so that he got only one more swipe in across the belly of the guy's wife so good and so goddamn deep that he was watching her guts spill out of her even as the guy's bloody fist descended and everything went suddenly black.

Hours later when it was over, when the ambulances had pulled away and the cops were finished and the busboys had mopped up the blood, when the glassier had patched the window with plywood and the gawking crowds were gone Diane was left alone at the bar waiting for Tasos, owner of the place and poor Theo's cousin, to come in from Westchester and assess all the damage.

The bottle of Absolute kept her company. The bottle was her buddy.

She drank and considered that she'd gotten to know the people in station two better than she'd ever wanted to.

She hadn't held out much hope for Mrs. Wolper but the medics felt differently. She'd make it, they thought. He hadn't managed to slash through any organs. But the Wolpers were going to have to put off their trip to Greece for quite a while. Danny Martino' burns were not serious and his friend John Walters had escaped the entire episode just by watering down his pants-leg. Likewise the Japanese couple, who'd done some fancy ducking. Hal Reese had died flooding the sidewalk with arterial blood. Jan Resnick's burns, cuts and bruises were stunningly lucky and superficial and would heal though she wasn't so sure about her heart. The woman had come completely unglued by the loss of the guy. She guessed they must have had something pretty damn special together.

Theo was badly cut and burned but he'd live.

Lindsey had been twenty-two years old. Diane had liked her.

She sat drinking her Absolut and thinking about Phil's last words to her just as the cops led him off to the squad car. Some weird shit about them sharing an apartment together.

She thought about her apartment. What she owed. The tips she didn't get tonight.

She lit another smoke and thought about the mob joint down in Little Italy.

Almost wondered if they were hiring.

Thanks to the folks at the Aegean, especially David and Carolyn.

When I was a kid in high school Thornton Wilder's *The Bridge of San Luis Rey* made a big and lasting impression on me and I've used his notion about the co-mingling of the fates of various strangers twice. First in *The Exit at Toledo Blade Boulevard*, which even mimicked Wilder's title, and here in "Station Two."

New York bars and restaurants are excellent places to observe people and their body-language—which often tells a story pretty clearly—and poor Jan and her bastard lover Hal were based on one such observation over nearly half an hour.

—JK

Elusive

The first time Kovelant stood in line for *Sleepdirt* was just before Halloween.

He didn't stand there long. It was raining cold and hard and the wind was high on 84th and his four-dollar umbrella wasn't up to protecting him from either. His face was wet and his shoes were practically swamped. The tickets were preview giveaways. Hence the line around the block. Kovelant decided to wait for the reviews and the release date and then maybe go. Ten bucks was ten bucks and free was free but pneumonia would cost him more than that in co-pays alone. He hailed a cab home and slipped *Dawn of the Dead* into the VCR and turned up the heat.

The second time was the weekend after Halloween and by then the reviews were in. *"A mini-masterpiece of terror,"* said the *New York Times*. *"The first real scare-the-hell-out-of-you horror movie since* Henry, Portrait of a Serial Killer," said the *Daily News*. *"Blacker than black!"* raved the *Post*.

He'd heard it all before but if you were a fan, you went. It was that simple.

So he stood in line—inside this time thank god, since this night was just as bad as the first one—at the Sony complex across the street and watched the SOLD OUT signs appear. *5:45. 8:00. 10:10.* The damn thing was a hit and this was New York City. He'd have to wait.

His life, such as it was, intruded and he didn't get to try again until early December. The intrusion came in the form of an old lover. Maggie was in town from Vermont on a first-ever Manhattan holiday shopping spree and intent on seeing sights, not horror movies. But the nice thing about writing was that he had the time to accompany her. They hit 5th Avenue and Madison for the shopping and the Planetarium, Rockefeller Center and the Metropolitan Museum for the sights. After dinner nights they hit the sack in Maggie's hotel. This with a lust uncommon for the Mags he'd known back in their hippie days despite the husband and pair of kids she was shopping for.

He put her in a cab to the airport on a Saturday night and Sunday he went to the movies.

There wasn't much of a line this time. The holiday feel-good blockbusters had weighed in solid competition. Waiting for the doors to open, *Sleepdirt* ticket finally clutched in hand Kovelant felt the slightest twinge in his lower back, a pinch, the sense of something bunching there so he shifted left and then right from the waist to loosen it up. When the line started moving a single step was all it took to shoot a white-knuckle bolt of pain off his hip and up into his neck and shoulder. A second step confirmed he was in trouble.

By the time he reached the nose-ringed quadruple-earpierced blonde collecting tickets the pain was an electric eel squirming throughout the entire right side of his body.

The girl handed him his stub. Then smiled.

"Hey, you're..."

"Jesus" he gasped. "I gotta sit."

He hoped the girl didn't think he meant he was jesus. Though he didn't much care either way.

The last aisle seat was empty so he took it. Normally he sat closer. Maybe he'd move up later, he thought.

Or maybe not.

Sitting was worse.

The eel had found its way into his head now. It felt like it was expanding there while at the same time constricting at his neck, forcing the neck down into his shoulders. The shoulders in turn seemed somehow to want to find their way into his lower back. The skin across his shoulders felt too tight for his goddamn body. He wasn't even sure he could get out of the damn seat but knew he'd better try. This just wasn't working. He gripped the armrests and thrust himself up. His right arm felt weak as a kitten.

Standing was better. *Not good*, but better.

The audience was still filing in so he moved slowly through and past them, afraid the slightest nudge might send him sprawling. At the entrance the ticket-girl smiled at him again.

"Popcorn's over that way," she said. "Men's room, that way. Hey listen, what's your name? I forget."

She sounded serious. He couldn't figure why in the world she would be. Did she think she knew him? He wasn't about to say *jesus* again though or anything else for that matter. He just wanted out of there.

Happily his apartment was right across the street. If he could get there.

What he wanted was a bed.

His doorman looked at him oddly. It didn't surprise him. He was practically bent in half by then. He took the elevator to the twenty-seventh floor.

And it was only when he'd dry-swallowed a handful of ibuprofen and got into that bed that he thought, *I can't believe it, I missed that movie again.* His GP, a neurologist, an MRI and two months of electrotherapy, ultrasound, cold and hot packs and various deep-muscle PT manipulations later, *Sleepdirt* was long out of the theatres but three months after that, available on tape. He rented a cassette from Tower Video. Took it home and popped in the VCR. Following the credit sequence, in which a screaming, bloody middle-aged man is being dragged by his legs into what appears to be a hotel laundry chute, he heard a crackling sound coming from the VCR and the screen went blank.

He hit EJECT on his remote and nothing happened. He did the same on the VCR proper. He opened the tape-port manually and tried pushing it, then lifting it out with his fingers. Finally he dug it out with a butter knife. Inside the cassette he could see a knot of mangled tape.

The following day he dropped it off at Tower Video and asked if he could replace it with another. The clerk punched it into his computer.

"We're out," he said. "Friday night. Movie's popular. We got DVDs in stock, though."

"I don't have a DVD player."

The guy looked at him as if he'd just announced he molested children.

"Try after the weekend. Wednesday, Thursday maybe. Slow days, y'know?"

Slow days for slow customers, he thought. Right.

On the way home he stopped at the Food Emporium. He bought some cheese and deli meats and a fresh loaf of rye. The pudgy little Spanish girl behind the counter practically had to stand on tiptoes to weigh the stack of bologna. He thought she had a pretty smile.

"Don't I know you?" she said.

"I don't think so."

"You look familiar."

"I come in a lot I guess. I'm right across the street."

"Yeah, probably that's it. Well, have a nice day."

"You too."

He worked on his book over the weekend and on Tuesday went back to Tower Video and picked up a copy of *Sleepdirt* on his credit slip for the first try. The clerk, a younger guy, eyebrow-pierced and shaved bald, looked up at him over his glasses and laughed.

"Checkin' yourself out, huh?"

"Excuse me?"

"Me, I thought you were terrific. Small part, sure, but you were great in it, man. Don't they give the actors copies? I thought they did."

"I'm not understanding you."

The clerk looked at him again more closely.

"That's not you?"

"What's not me?"

"In the movie? I mean, man, you could pass for his twin brother."

"I don't have a twin brother."

"See, I thought you were this actor, this guy in the movie. *Amazing* death scene. Absolutely *beautiful.* I can't believe you're not him. Sorry, man."

He handed him the plastic yellow bag.

"You have a good day."

Kovelant walked out shaking his head. Now that was interesting. Maybe it explained the ticket-taker at the Sony complex and the counter girl at the Food Emporium. Now that he thought of it he'd even been aware lately of getting looks on the street a bit more often than his less-than-perfect features might ordinarily compel in passers-by.

He had a look-alike in this elusive movie here. How about that?

He put *Sleepdirt* in the VCR and turned on the television and prepared to settle in.

Nothing.

No sound, no picture.

Nothing at all.

He checked the wall plug and the connections and both were fine. He unplugged the set and plugged it in again. He unplugged it a second time and plugged in the clock-radio instead. The clock ran perfectly. He called Manhattan Cable and after twenty minutes of recorded music learned that there were no transmission problems in his area, *thank you very much for calling.*

His television had suddenly died on him. *Shit!*

And he thought finally, *what the hell is it with this movie?*

"I think it's jinxed," he told Maggie later.

Since her trip to New York they'd taken to phoning more often. He wondered what her husband thought about that or if he knew. He could hear her pull on the joint on the other end of the line. He'd given up the stuff years ago.

"I haven't seen it," she said.

"That's the point. Neither have I."

He heard her exhale and then there was silence for a while.

"Maybe it's like dreams."

"Huh?"

"You know. You know how they say movies are like dreams?"

"Who says movies are like dreams?"

"They do. Except they're mass dreams, not individual ones. We sit in a theatre and have this...*dream* together. And this actor, he's supposed to look just like you, right? Could almost be your twin brother."

"Yeah. So?"

"He dies in it, right?"

"Right."

"Well, they also say you can't see yourself *die* in a dream. That you always wake up first right *before* you die. That you have to."

It was the common wisdom.

"So you're saying..."

"That you can't see the movie because you can't see yourself die in it. I mean, maybe in some way it is you. Not some look-alike."

"I think I'd know it if I were in a movie. I think my checkbook would know it too."

He could almost hear her shrug but her voice had that playful tone to it.

"More things in heaven and earth, Hieronymus..."

"Mags, honey, you've got two kids to take care of and a husband to feed every night. You tripping again?"

"Of course not. Though probably my kids are. Wouldn't be surprised."

"Just finish a Stephen King book, by any chance?"

"Nope. Tell you what I'll do. You sit tight. I've got a little mom-and-pop video store just a few blocks away. I'll go over and rent the thing. I mean, so far nobody's told me I look like anybody in what's it called? *Sleepwalk?*"

"*Sleepdirt.*"

"Whatever. Anyway, I'll check it out for you. Richard will think I'm nuts, but..."

He needed to shop for a new TV set anyway. Check out *Consumer Reports.*

"Okay, why not. Go for it."

"I'll pick it up tomorrow. I can watch it tomorrow night."

"It's supposed to be a rough one, Mags. I know how you feel about these things. I'd stay off the dope if I were you."

"If you stay off the sauce. I'll call you, sweets."

And she did. Two nights later the phone rang. He knew it was her even before he answered.

"Sorry, but Richard and I got into it night before last so I only just watched it now."

"Anything you want to talk about?"

"You mean Richard? No, we're okay now. I *think.* The movie, though..."

"What about it?"

"Well, it was rough, all right."

"I figured. Sorry."

"That's okay. You warned me. But that actor? The one who looks like you? My god! does he ever! I could have sworn it was you. Even the voice is the same. And you know that slouch you have? The posture thing I'm always on your case for? Well..."

"How does he die, Mags?" *He suddenly had to know.*

"Jesus! That part's awful. He..."

He heard static.

The line went dead.

"Mags? Can you hear me? Mags? Shit!"

He hung up and dialed again. Busy. Maybe she was trying to call him, he thought. He hung up the phone and waited. A minute passed. Two. He dialed again and got another busy signal. She was not the type for a cell phone and he'd never bothered to get her e-mail address. He hated e-mail. Now he wished he had.

Two hours later it was past midnight and he'd tried a dozen times or more and every time it was busy. He'd even asked an operator to check and see if there were problems on the line. She said the line was in use, period. Who the hell was Maggie talking to? *If anybody.* He had lurid fantasies of her husband strangling her with the phone cord in a sudden jealous rage.

He didn't know Richard. It was possible.

But highly improbable. No, that wasn't it.

You are not meant to see this movie, he thought.

And then he thought, *ridiculous, the hell you're not* and went to bed, resolved.

The following day he was up early, before nine o'clock—unusual for him—and by ten he was out the door. It was cold and dark and snow looked likely. He found a cab on Broadway. At Circuit City he made the purchase of an RCA Colortrak television set with a sixteen inch screen, a Panasonic Progressive Scan DVD player, and a Panasonic Omnivision VCR—though as far as he knew there was nothing wrong with the old one. He paid an additional $72.50 for same-day delivery and installation.

When the technician had everything hooked up and explained to him the mysteries of DVD technology—it took a while—he got on his coat and hat and headed through a light dusting of snow for Tower Video. There were six rental copies of *Sleepdirt* available on tape. He guessed it was a slow day. He piled them into his basket. There were ten rental copies available on DVD. He took them too.

There were twenty on DVD for sale and another dozen on tape. He took all of them. By the time he got to the checkout counter he was grinning.

The girl looked at him strangely.

"Wow," she said, "you must really *like* this movie."

"I haven't seen it yet."

It was as though she hadn't heard him.

"I never seen nobody do nothing like *this* before. Always a first time though, right?"

"You got that," he said. "Always a first time."

She rang him up. *Gotcha,* he thought and walked out the door. *Gotcha now you sonovabitch.*

It occurred to him that there was a Barnes & Noble across the street and that they sold DVDs too and even though the bag was heavy and he hadn't done much hauling since his back went out and snow was blowing in his face he figured better safe than sorry and was halfway across the northbound lane of Broadway when the bag split open at the seam going suddenly light in his hand and tapes and DVDs clattered to the pavement like a fallen sack of old dry bones and he stooped to pick them up.

"Oh, come on," Richard said. "You're watching that thing again? It's disgusting."

"I know it's disgusting," Maggie said. "It's a horror movie. It's supposed to be scary and disgusting. But when's the last time you saw somebody who looks *exactly like somebody you know* get his head torn off by a New York City bus? In slo-mo no less. Tell me that."

Her husband left the room.

She watched the actor whose name was Kevin something stoop down in the middle of the street and hit the SLOW button on the DVD remote so that now it was running frame-by-frame. Even after half a dozen viewings she couldn't see how they got the shot so damn realistic. Usually you could spot some FX giveaway even with what computers could do these days. Richard was right—*that was one of their problems, he was always right*—and it was ghoulish of her, she knew. But there was Kovelant. His spitting image.

And there was his head.

And then it wasn't there anymore where it should have been—it was sailing through the air off toward the camera, almost directly *into* the camera, a mashed, twisted, gore-soaked version of his face, and the bus raced by, and the body that, dressed at least, looked exactly like the body she'd slept beside and screwed every way to Sunday gouting blood all along the snowy street.

She wondered why he'd hung up on her. Why he hadn't called her back. Why he hadn't answered *her* calls.

She wondered if he'd finally seen the movie.

Right now though—darkly, almost guiltily fascinated—she mostly wondered *how in hell* they got that scene.

L ike a lot of other old wives' tales that turn out to be true, in my own experience and those of everybody I've ever talked to, you can't see your death in a dream. Why this should be so—when you can dream anything wildly horrific short of that, when you can dream falling out of a plane or making love to Betty Friedan or Richard Nixon or the neighborhood cat—remains a mystery.

It's been pointed out by many that movies are a lot like manufactured dreams. You see them projected in front of you, usually in the dark, you can't control their contents god knows and when they're over, though they may linger, they're over.

I thought maybe you can't see yourself die in a movie either.

The title of this particular movie, *Sleepdirt*, was the name of a late Frank Zappa album. A little inside joke. "Sleep dirt" being a euphemism for the contents of your nightly bedpan.

—JK

Papa

"You're him, right? You're Papa."

My god. *Papa again.* People had commented on the resemblance before, plenty of times. But nobody had ever accused McPheeters of actually *being* him. That was a new one. He put his scotch down on the bar and smiled at the guy and shook his head.

The guy thought he was Hemingway.

Never mind that he had a foot plus in height on old Ernie. Never mind that he outweighed him by fifty pounds at his heaviest.

Hell, never mind that Hemingway was forty years dead.

Elvis sightings were common. Hemingway sightings, he guessed, somewhat less so.

He assumed the guy was drunk. You could never tell a drunk much of anything but he figured he'd give it a shot.

" 'Fraid not. Folks do tell me that I look like him now and then, though."

The guy laughed and drained his screwdriver. McPheeters noticed that his thin bony hands were shaking. It could have been the booze. It could have been that the guy really thought he was in the presence of greatness. Long dead greatness.

"Bull. You can't fool me with that accent. You can throw me that Gomer Pyle stuff all you want. You're him."

Gomer Pyle? He wondered exactly what kind of time warp this guy was living in. Did he even know he was sitting in a bar on the Upper West Side of New York and not down in sunny Key West?

"Hell, I've read all your stuff. *Farewell to Arms, For Whom the Bell Tolls, A Moveable Feast, Death in the Afternoon, The Green Hills of Africa*—I mean, all of it. Even read that play of yours, *The Fifth*

Column. You're pretty fuckin' good, you know that? Not as good as Chandler was but hey, who is? So why'd you quit?"

"I died."

He laughed. "Right. And I'm Elvis Presley. You'd died, I'da heard about it."

He didn't look like Elvis Presley. He looked like he worked on Wall Street and it had been a pretty rough day over at the Stock Exchange. The tie was askew, the shirt rumpled underneath the bright suspenders.

The guy leaned over and held out his hand. "Mike Kelly. Pleased to meetcha."

McPheeters shook it. "Neal McPheeters. Likewise." Kelly laughed again. "Hey, whatever you say, man. Whatever name you're goin' by. Fine with me."

McPheeters reflected that in all these years it had never come remotely *this* far. This guy Kelly was either way drunk, putting him on, crazy or quite a character.

Or all of the above.

It's New York, he thought. *You never know what you're going to meet or where.*

At least the guy was a reader.

Kelly slid off his stool and directly onto the one next to McPheeters'. McPheeters sipped his scotch. He wasn't sure he cared for the intimacy. Maybe he'd best just drink up and get out of here. There were plenty of bars.

Kelly glanced at the bartender. He'd been doing that. The bartender was a looker. McPheeters didn't blame him.

"What'd you think of the movies, you don't mind my asking?"

"Movies?"

"The ones from the books. Tracy was great in *Old Man and the Sea,* I thought, and I liked George C. Scott in *Islands in the Stream.* Scott even looked like you a little, you know? But Tyrone Power was a complete and utter *wuss* in *Sun Also Rises.* I mean, Tyrone fuckin' Power! Jesus!"

"Ava Gardner was pretty good, though."

"Oh yeah, Ava Gardner. She was fine."

"Flynn too."

"You're right. Errol Flynn. Him too. Hey, you ever fuck Gertrude Stein?"

He laughed. "Did *anybody* ever fuck Gertrude Stein?"

"Gotta figure Toklas, right?"

It was kind of fun, playing along with the guy like this. Made for an unusual Saturday afternoon. He didn't really want to go back to the painting anyway. The studio felt small and cramped today. Probably it was the goddamn deadline pushing at him. He hated deadlines and he hated being pushed. Painters were supposed to take their own sweet time. And the warm autumn sunlight was sharp and crisp through the big plate-glass windows.

What the hell. He'd order another. He raised a hand to get the bartender's attention.

Kelly must have read his mind. "Hey listen, forget the scotch. It is scotch you drink, right? Thought so. You know what I got over at my place?"

"Your place?"

"My apartment." He leaned in close and whispered. "I've got abs."

"Huh?"

"Abs. Absinthe. You still drink absinthe now and then, doncha? I know you guys put away crates of it in Spain and Paris. Of course it's illegal here. Damned if I know why. I order it off the internet. Czech stuff, UK distributor. One hundred twenty proof. Great stuff."

He'd never tried absinthe. He'd always wondered about it too. What painter wouldn't? *The Green Fairy. The Green Muse.* The favored drink of Manet, Degas, Lautrec, Van Gogh, Gauguin and Picasso, not to mention writers as diverse as Baudelaire and Oscar Wilde, Mark Twain and Rimbaud, Poe and Whitman. And here he was being offered some. Another first.

"We'll go over to my place. Three blocks away. Shoot the shit about the old days. What do you say?"

He didn't know this guy from Adam. But he didn't look much like a serial killer either. And McPheeters towered over him. Anyhow it was a nice day for a stroll. Absinthe went all the way back to the Greeks and Egyptians for chrissake. The game got tired, he'd end it and head on back to the bar.

"Sure, why not?"

"Been a while, right?"

"Yep. Been a while."

The apartment was a third-floor walkup on 74th Street just off Columbus. Not what he expected. He'd expected a high-rise.

"What exactly you do for a living, Mike?" he said.

"Science fiction editor. Del Rey Books."

Maybe that explained a few things and maybe it didn't. Kelly unlocked the door and they stepped inside. It was a good-sized one-bedroom, not too clean, nice furnishings but undistinguished except for the fact that pretty much every available surface was piled with books, galleys, manuscripts. Even the computer had books perched precariously on top of it. Kelly moved some off the couch and an armchair facing it across the cluttered table. If there was a woman in this guy's life McPheeters couldn't find her anywhere.

"Have a seat. Make yourself at home. *Mi casa es su casa.*"

McPheeters took the couch.

"All right if I smoke?"

"You smoke? Damn, I didn't remember that. Sure, light up. I'll find you an ashtray and get the stuff."

He disappeared into the kitchen. McPheeters lit a Camel.

In a moment Kelly came back again with an ashtray and a book and cleared a spot for the ashtray and handed him the book. *Absinthe: History in a Bottle*, by Barnaby Conrad III.

"Check it out," he said. "I'll be right back."

The book was expensive, beautifully illustrated and designed. Many of the prints he was familiar with. Van Gogh's *Night Café in Arles*. Degas *L'Absinthe*—which had caused so much stir in England. Manet's *The Absinthe Drinker*. A photo of Verlaine caught his eye. The poet was sitting in a tavern with a full glass in front of him and a bottle on the table, his eyes defining the phrase "blind drunk," as though wholly in the thrall of some inner vision. And there was Oscar Wilde, looking quite the dandy, with a quote on the "three stages" of absinthe.

"The first stage is like ordinary drinking," he read, *"the second when you begin to see monstrous and cruel things, but if you persevere you will enter upon the third stage where you see things you want to see, wonderful curious things."*

But he didn't want to read about the stuff. He didn't want somebody else's perceptions distorting his own. He wanted a feel for this first-hand.

He closed the book. Kelly walked back into the room smiling and bearing a tarnished metal serving tray. On the tray was a clear squarish half-full bottle of bright green liquid, a plastic bottle of Poland Spring water, a bowl piled with sugar cubes, a slotted spoon, two highball glasses and a small bowl of ice. He set it on the table and pulled up his chair.

"Sebar Absinthe," he said. "I don't know how you take it. Sebar doesn't louche all that well but I refrigerate it and that helps."

"Louche?"

"C'mon, man. *Louche*, cloud over. Emerald to opal, remember? The ice helps too but I don't use ice in mine." He figured he wouldn't either.

Kelly uncorked the bottle and poured.

"So what's it gonna be?"

McPheeters shrugged. "The usual."

"Good. Me too. Be my guest."

"You're the host, Mike. You first."

"Okay."

He watched Kelly take a sugar cube and place it on the slotted spoon.

"The UK distributors? They send you one of these little spoons with every order. Nice touch I think."

He balanced the spoon across the rim and cracked the seal on the Poland water, dribbled a little over the sugar cube and watched as the sugar melted and began to cloud the liquor below—*emerald to opal*—waited and poured again and then finally a third time until the cube dissolved away.

McPheeters repeated the procedure and drank. The taste was herbal, almost musty, bitter despite the sugar and with a high anise aroma—like an ouzo that had maybe sat in somebody's closet too long. Not unpleasant but not the tastiest stuff that had ever passed his lips either.

"So what do you think?'

"Not bad."

"Not what you're used to, I know, but..."

The guy was apologizing. McPheeters was used to Dewars and the very occasional single-malt.

"Like I say, not bad."

Only three sips and already he was beginning to feel it. Maybe it was the scotch it was riding on top of but he doubted that. The stuff was strong.

"Tell me the truth, uh, *Neal*—you really like Picasso? I never could warm up to the guy."

That was a topic he could speak to at least.

"Your question's too broad, Mike. You've got to say *which* Picasso. The main thing about Picasso is he kept reinventing himself. He never did one thing for very long. In the blue period he's interested in Lautrec and Rusinol, in the Iberian, Cezanne, in the cubist, Braque. His subject matter's all the hell over the place, from war in Spain to harlequins and clowns. He did collage and lithography and ceramics and bronzes, not just paintings."

"Okay, okay, which period, then? Which you like best?"

"Post-cubism. *Guernica*. No question."

And then he wanted to know about Dos Passos. McPheeters had read Dos Passos so he indulged him on that one too. They poured a second glass. And what did he think of Faulkner?

"I never met him."

He almost laughed out loud. He was having too much fun with this. This was getting crazy.

"I liked his books, though."

"Really? I thought you hated that long windy shit."

"Not if it's good long windy shit. Can't say much for Proust, though."

And then there was a good long lag in the conversation which McPheeters was grateful for while they both just let the liquor work in them, Kelly leaning back in the chair staring out the window toward the fire escape sipping at his drink and McPheeters flipping through the book again, turning pages at random. Photos of a wormwood harvest and the Pernod distillery with great bags of it dried and stored in the basement, a drawing of a brain infected with meningitis, a French cartoon from 1910 called *The Absinthe Demon*—a massive leering woman hovering behind a sad-eyed young man with a half-empty glass beside him on the table—a label inspired by the 1894 Dreyfus Affair of a brand called Absinthe Anti-Jew with the legend *France for the French*, another photo of a Pernod factory at Pontarlier which had been converted into a

World War I field hospital, the beds all made of stacked absinthe crates, the gaunt haunted faces of the injured staring out at the photographer.

"Interesting book, Mike," he said finally.

"Huh?"

"The book. Interesting."

"Sure. Hey, pour us another."

Kelly sounded as though he was feeling irritable all of a sudden. McPheeters wasn't. The colors in the book and even in the drab room were leaping out at him, practically assaulting his old tired eyes and the effect was delightful. He'd taken THC once—a synthetic cannabis, almost though not quite a hallucinogen—and this was similar. He'd have one more drink and then go for a walk, he thought. Central Park ought to be just right for this stuff.

He poured one for himself and another for Kelly and slid Kelly's across the table.

"You're a real pain in the ass, you know that?" Kelly said.

"What?"

"You. You're a real pain in the ass. All that bullfighting, hunting, fishing bullshit. Like I'm really supposed to believe you carried some soldier into the trenches with Austrian shrapnel and bullets in your legs in one war and that you were first to enter Paris during the next. Right. Like you drink a quart of booze a day. Right. Like you're so damn courageous and cool under pressure, not like your buddies, not like poor Thompson—whatsisname, Karl in *The Green Hills of Africa*—who you say's so selfish and mean-spirited and who you barely even bother to disguise. Your old buddy, y'know? Your old drinking buddy from Sloppy Joe's. Poor bastard.

"You treat him like shit. You treat your wives like shit too. Every one of them. You marry Hadley for her fucking trust fund and then cheat on her with Pauline and abandon your kid and marry Pauline because she's got an Uncle Gus with plenty of cash to hand you and then dump her with two kids because you're fucking around with Martha and then you dump Martha after making a complete ass of her in *Across the River and Into the Trees* but at least there are no kids with that one, right? and then there's Mary, and you cheat on her with Adriana. What the hell is it with you? You got to keep your dick wet all the time?"

McPheeters gulped down the rest of his drink. Okay, he had it now. The guy was nuts. The guy was practically giving off sparks.

He'd only married twice, actually.

It was time to go. Game over.

He set down his glass and stood up and so did Kelly. "Look Mike, I tried to tell you. I'm not Papa. Papa's long gone."

It was like he didn't hear him.

"And *then* what do you do? You let your granddaughters do those fucking movies! You let 'em both get naked for godsakes! You let Margeaux get raped in that piece of shit *Lipstick* and Mariel get raped and fucking blown away stark naked in *Star 80.* What the hell were you thinking of? That's *family,* man! Don't you have any sense of responsibility? Are you out of your goddamn *mind?*"

McPheeters sighed and turned toward the door.

As he'd noted before, you couldn't tell a drunk much of anything.

"Thanks for the drinks, Mike. It's been interesting."

"YOU OUGHT TO BLOW YOUR FUCKING HEAD OFF! JUST LIKE YOUR FATHER DID, YOU SONOVABITCH!"

He thought he'd give it one more try.

"I did, Mike. I did just that."

In Central Park the trees were every bit as green as the absinthe was until after a couple of hours it started to wear off and the world went real again.

He walked back to the studio and started painting.

Thanks to P.D. Cacek

This story was written for a doomed *Absinthe* anthology which I readily agreed to after having tasted the stuff in far too large a dosage one night at a writer's conference a few years back. I was told the following day by P. D. Cacek that at some point I simply disappeared and some other guy—an agreeable guy but certainly not me—took over. I did a panel discussion at noon that day and though I'm told I spoke well and at some length I don't remember any of that either.

You meet a number of more or less crazy people in bars, absinthe-addled or not—and my good friend, the painter Neal McPheeters, does look a bit like Papa Hemingway. Especially after I've had a couple.

—JK

The Fountain

She stepped out of the scent of roses, snapdragons, carnations and babies' breath into the rank steamy summer afternoon. She missed the shop's air-conditioning almost immediately. What she did not miss were Gordon's silences. They had sold mostly roses and lilies this morning and he was acting as though it were her fault—when it was simply their customers' customary lack of imagination. Give her a delphinium over a lily any day.

But she was leaving those silences behind for a while, thank you very much.

His problem was not with sales anyway. His problem was with her.

And what about mine with you? she thought.

She walked the two blocks to Columbus Gourmet and ordered a grilled chicken sandwich to go—whole wheat bread, extra mayo, hold the pickle. Took a half-liter bottle of Poland Spring from the cooler and paid and then she was on the street again headed for the Park.

She passed the Olcott and the Mayfair and the Dakota, in front of which a uniformed guard who looked barely old enough to drink in a New York bar was pointing out to a pair of tourist girls—probably for the billionth time—the exact spot John Lennon had been shot by Mark David Chapman on December 8, 1980.

The girls looked horrified, as though it had happened only days ago.

At 72nd Street she crossed Central Park West past the hot dog and ice cream vendors and into Strawberry Fields. A sleeping young bearded man sprawled along a bench, his guitar hugged to his chest like a lover. Nannies sat and chatted in the shade.

In the center of the *Imagine* mosaic lay a single fresh yellow long-stem rose. A *yellow rose meant joy and friendship*. She wondered if Yoko Ono had ordered it placed there, perhaps on a daily basis—if that were her signal flower for him. It was possible. Tourists snapped low-angle photos of each other crouched behind the mosaic, respectful, unsmiling.

She walked down Olmstead's shady gently sloping hill. Smelled fresh-cut grass and moist earth. She cut past the statue of Daniel Webster down to the sidewalk along Park Drive and saw the bikers and joggers out in number each in their solitary dedication and a man on roller-blades with a cell-phone to his ear.

The sky was hazy over Bethesda Fountain—the thick green Ramble beyond the lake in the distance rendered almost impressionistic by the weight of summer air. She walked down the first set of eighteen steps to the landing, empty but for a pair of Hispanic lovers in oblivious embrace and four young boys who at first glance seemed to be playing some sort of game.

As she crossed the landing she saw it was not a game—not exactly.

Not according to her notion of the word.

Of the four boys only one of them was fat and so was the paperback they were tossing back and forth, keeping it away from him, its pages fluttering through the air sounding like the wings of startled pigeons, slapping into the hands of first one boy and then another while they laughed—cruelly she thought—at the fat boy's clear distress. She wondered how long the binding was going to hold out. If they'd quit before the book fell apart entirely.

Little boys can be such bastards, she thought as she descended the second steep set of stairs. She crossed the Terrace to the lip of the Fountain and sat and uncapped the water and unwrapped the sandwich.

Men too.

The wind shifted at her back and a brief gentle misting of spray off the blue stone lower basin drifted across her face. She turned to gaze up a moment at the bronze angel above it, bestowing blessings on the waters. In the 1880's the sculptor—a woman, unusual for the time—had used the metaphor of the biblical angel of Bethesda, whose touch disturbing the waters of a Jerusalem sheep-market pool could cure the first sick person who entered it, to celebrate the delivery of clean pure water off the Croton.

She took a bite of her sandwich. Chased it with a sip of Poland Spring. On the platform the boys were playing a running game now—still keep-away, but tossing the book less and dodging the fat boy's attempt to grab for it instead. Perhaps they were preserving the binding. For the fat boy it was still hopeless.

The Hispanic lovers were moving arm in arm down the second set of stairs.

She envied them. There were no men in her own life and hadn't been for quite a while. Only Gordon—who evidently thought he had lover potential, anyway. At least as of Monday night.

She wondered how in hell he'd arrived at that idea.

She'd been counting the cash in the till just after closing because Gordon hated doing that for some reason even though it was his shop, and he'd been stowing plants in the walk-in cooler for the night when suddenly she felt his hand in her hair, moving gently back and forth along the side of her head.

She laughed and said *what are you doing, Gordon? I'll screw up the count.*

But he didn't stop.

He'd never so much as touched her before.

He took one step toward her and then two and when he pressed up against her ass and she felt how hard he was she threw the cash back into the drawer and turned and put her hand to his chest and shoved him. He damn near went into the cooler.

She picked up her purse and slammed her way out the door.

In the three days since there'd been nothing but silence between them unless speech was absolutely necessary and she wondered how long it could go on like this. She needed the job of course. New York was woefully short on jobs these days. With both her parents gone she was struggling to put her younger sister through her third year at CUNY. She needed the money.

But what he'd done was harassment pure and simple. She knew that if he ever tried anything again, she'd have to quit.

She'd thought he was a friend.

And she was considering this when she saw the book sail over the platform and down the stairs and then the boy, the fat boy, flailing his arms silently and tumbling down after it, heard his outstretched arm snap like a pistol shot and then a cry that she could only describe later as a loud whimper and was not aware of dropping the sandwich or of standing but only of that other sound he made at the bottom, like an axe into a treetrunk as the back of his head cracked against the clean white Terrace.

It was the young Hispanic man who first performed CPR on the boy while his lover looked on and then, moments later, the emergency crew. A crowd had gathered, among them the three boys who stared on in shock and all of whom were crying to one degree or another. They hadn't pushed him, it was an accident, he'd simply lost his balance and fell—two elderly black women had seen the whole thing from the top the second staircase. *Jesus, just a kid* she heard a man say behind her and then a woman's voice, almost a whisper. *Such a shame. So much to look forward to.*

She was interviewed by the two policemen along with a few others sitting by the Fountain who'd seen pretty much what she'd seen. By the time they were finished the ambulance had long since pulled away. The ambulance was pro forma by now anyway. Eighteen steps is a long way to fall down an incline as steep as that and the boy was dead practically the minute he hit the Terrace.

The book, as it turned out, was Stephen King's *Hearts in Atlantis.*

Behind her the waters of Bethesda Fountain trickled incessantly into the clear clean pool. She still was shaking. She picked up her fallen sandwich, her white paper bag and bottled water and dropped them into a trashcan and went back the way she came.

Someone had removed the yellow rose from the *Imagine* mosaic.

A yellow rose meant joy and friendship.

She couldn't believe it. It had happened that quickly. The rose was gone.

She opened the door to the flower shop and Gordon was glowering at her from behind the desk. She was very late. She wasn't about to tell him why. He started to speak but she held up her hand and stopped him.

She said, *I quit.*

One bright summer morning at Bethesda Fountain I saw some boys playing a dangerous game of monkey-in-the-middle at the top of the stairs. Where the hell were their parents? I thought. This kid in the middle could be dead by noon. It segued into the idea that life is sometimes brutally short and not to be wasted.

—JK

Do You Love Your Wife?

"Sometimes I feel like you're...I don't know, not really *there* anymore," she said. "Like no matter what I do, it wouldn't make any difference, would it. Know what I mean?"

They were lying in bed. He was tired and a little buzzed from the scotches after work. Greene's *The Power and the Glory* lay open on her lap. He was halfway through Stone's *Bay of Souls*.

She was right. Stone could obviously rouse himself. He could not.

She was heading to California in a few days, leaving behind the chill of New York and his own chill for a week or so. Her ex-lover beckoned. Perhaps he'd become her lover all over again. Bass hadn't asked.

"I'm not complaining," she said. "I'm not criticizing. You know that."

"I know."

"And it's not just you and me. Seems like it's everything. You used to write. Hell, you used to paint. It's not like you."

"It's like *part* of me obviously."

"Not the best part."

"Well. Maybe not."

She didn't say the rest of it. *Even after three whole years it's still her isn't it*. She hadn't the slightest urge to hurt him with it. She was simply observing and leaving him an opening should he wish to talk. He didn't. It wasn't precisely the loss of Annabel that was bothering him these days anyhow. It was what was left of him in her absence. Which seemed to amount to less and less—a subtle yet distinct difference. He continued to feel himself rolling far beneath the white-water wake of their parting. Way down where the water was still and deep and very thin.

"Confront her," Gary said.

"Annabel?"

"Yes, Annabel. Who else?"

"After all this time?"

"My point exactly. You're not getting any younger."

"It's easier said than done. She's married now, remember?"

"So are you and Laura. In your very odd way."

He was referring to Laura seeing her old lover again.

Gary didn't approve and didn't mind saying so. It was four in the morning. They were closing *The Gates of Hell*. It was a hot summer night and the thirtysomething crew had come at them fast and furious despite the nine-dollar well-drinks.

"Confront both of them then, what the hell."

"I don't even know him. We met once when she was bartending for all of about five minutes. I'm not sure I'd recognize him if he were sitting right in front of me."

"So maybe that's part of the problem. You don't know the guy. So you don't know what he offers her. You don't know *why him*. I mean, sometimes you meet the other guy and he's not all that much, you know? Brings *her* down a notch. Sometimes that's just what you need.

"You miss her and you think you're missing this...enormous personality. But you're only seeing her in the context of the two of you. You've got no perspective. You're in there yourself, churning things up. Messing with the perspective. You think you know somebody but you don't—not until you either live with them or see them in some whole new situation, like with somebody else...That's my take on it, anyway. And I still think you're fucking crazy letting Laura fly away to some clown in California."

He ignored the last bit. He couldn't tell Laura what to do and wouldn't want to anyway. He had to figure that she knew what she was doing.

But he thought it possible that Gary might be on to something regarding Annabel. When she left she'd insisted on cutting him off completely. No phone calls, no e-mails, no letters. A clean break she called it. He remembered wincing at the raw cliché.

At first he didn't believe she was capable of such draconian thinking—not when it came to them—so he tried anyway. But it became apparent that no confrontation, no follow-up of any sort short of appearing at her apartment was about to happen.

He knew where *that* little visit would lead. Access to her home was by invitation only. It would only earn him the humiliation of having a door once wide open to him slammed shut in his face.

The very last e-mail she'd sent him was calm and deliberate—informing him that she'd thrown out all her photos of them and suggesting he do the same. That it would speed up the healing process. Yet another cliché but he let it pass. Three months later she'd married a guy she'd known and dated off and on for a long time before they met and that was the last he'd heard of her.

He'd been angry, hurt and surprised over both developments. First the cut-off and then the marriage. But there was to be no court of appeals nor any use howling in the wind. It had seemed intolerable to simply stop, to surrender all communication. For a while Bass damn near hated her.

Yet three years later he felt no anger anymore. He could only wonder where it had gone. Because back then *you'll get over it in time* along with *making a clean break of it* and *speeding up the healing process* had seemed the father, son, and holy ghost of useless psychobabble. They disgusted and infuriated him.

But maybe in the long run they'd obtained after all. *Victory through inanity.*

Because here he was.

Curious in a passive sort of way about what if anything could possibly wake his dead ass up again, resurrect his sense of engagement in Life After Annabel. But the operative word was still *passive.* Confrontation? Three years ago, in a minute. But now he wasn't even sure he had the energy anymore. It was possible that the time for explanation and understanding and that most odious of all suspender-and-bowtied words *closure* had simply come and gone.

He'd never thrown out his own photos.

So he went through them for the first time in a long time over a corned beef on rye for lunch the following day. He felt a brief twinge looking at them. The pinch of a muscle you could stretch a moment later and be rid of.

Still it was something.

He decided to search her out on the net. He'd thought of doing that before but resisted it, wary of any further humiliation.

He punched in her maiden name and got nothing. Then tried her married name What came back was a single photo. A wedding picture two and a half years old—Annabel and her husband Gerard standing smiling beneath a canopy of healthy green palm-fronds in front of some old New Orleans hotel. Annabel looking lovely in a pale green shoulderless gown, her husband slightly shorter than she and balding, wearing a white silk short-sleeved shirt, lopsided grin and a crisp new Panama hat. She gazed not at the camera but into the sky. And that was exactly like her. Annabel was a painter and the sky was her true north, her canvas.

It was the only thing familiar.

The caption read INTRODUCING MR. AND MRS. GERARD POPE. AT MARDI GRAS. LOOK WHAT WE WENT AND DID!

The photo was off her husband's website. Bass had no reason to think he even had one. No idea that what he did for a living was write detective novels—fairly successful ones from the look of it. He roamed the site. Book-covers and reviews and a bibliography and message board and quotes from *Publishers Weekly* and Lawrence Block. Not too shabby at all. He had a series character who'd appeared first in six paperback originals and then more recently in two hardcovers, presumably with paperbacks forthcoming.

There was that twinge again.

Possibly the twinge was jealousy. Bass had seriously hoped to write one day himself—the bartending was supposed to have been temporary.

Or perhaps it was the fact that she and Bass had talked about New Orleans together too, while the farthest south they'd ever gotten was Cape May in the spring their very first year...

But more likely he was beginning to experience what Gary had talked about.

Context.

Here she was, Annabel embraced within the photo. Another, different Annabel. Far beyond the scope or influence of that entity which had once been Annabel and Bass together. With a man he barely recognized, to all purposes a total stranger. And in this man's presence—on that day at least—she was happy.

So it seemed that she could be perfectly happy without him.

He'd known that of course. Any cerebrum worth its salt could fire up that conclusion. But he thought the twinge came not from there but from some less apollonian area of the brain. The part men shared with snakes and birds and dinosaurs. That part which holds a single thing above all self-evident—*eat or be eaten*. Take or be taken.

Just a twinge.

But enough so that when a few days later Laura smiled and kissed him goodbye at the door to their apartment and lugged her bags downstairs to the taxi headed for LaGuardia, it began—unexpectedly—to move from twinge to throb. To leak through into this brand-new *second* void in his life created by her absence like a beaver-dam broken slowly apart by a heavy upstream rain.

Its immediate focus was Gerard, not Annabel. Which seemed strange to him because website aside he had no idea who Gerard even was. Bass bought one of his paperbacks but he hated thrillers so beyond reading the first few pages to ascertain that the man was capable of handling line and paragraph with more than meager skill he delved no further. So how could he feel such a growing *animus*—because that's what it was—toward somebody he'd never shaken hands with? Whose habits, tastes, voice, wit *or lack of wit* he knew nothing of?

How could you begin to dislike what amounted to a human abstraction?

Good question, he thought.

But his dream-life wasn't asking.

And Gerard was beginning to show up there on a pretty regular basis.

In one dream he and Gerard were trying to decipher blurred-out cooking directions printed on a bag of frozen food—some kind of stuffed Italian bread. They needed to know the oven time and couldn't read the damn thing. It was very frustrating.

In another they were playing chess. Pieces kept disappearing. A pawn here, a bishop there. Bass suspected himself of cheating.

In yet another they were seated beneath a shade-tree in Central Park watching a little girl play on the monkey bars and the little girl was Annabel. This did not seem strange to either of them. Bass lit a Winston and inhaled and Gerard leaned over smiling and plucked it from his lips and tossed it. Annabel laughed and jumped off the monkey bars and crushed it underfoot. Bass was furious with both of them.

Then there was the really bad one.

There's Gerard, seated in front of an old bare country-style oak table, massive, and he's tied to a heavy wooden armchair. His legs are tied to the chair-legs and his arms are tied to the chair-arms. Annabel is nowhere to be seen. Gerard stares at Bass, his brow furrowed with anxiety. Bass asks him, do you love your wife? *He nods in the affirmative.*

Then suddenly there's Annabel, similarly tied to a similar chair at the other end of the table. Behind her is a screen door open to the starry night. Moths drift through the doorway, attracted by the light. A luna moth, the color of her wedding dress, settles on the knuckles of her right hand where it grips the chair. Bass brushes it away and his carving-knife immediately replaces it, big and sharp and elegant in its way and poised to sever all four fingers and maybe the thumb too for good measure.

He asks Gerard again do you love your wife? *and presses the knife gently to her flesh.*

He nods yes and Bass sees that he is gagged now, as is she.

Bass lifts the knife off her fingers and transfers it to Gerard's right hand and asks him a third time, do you love your wife? *and he nods again slowly, sadly it seems, almost a polite bow to him and full of understanding. He reaches over to place his free hand on top of the knife and push suddenly down and the screams behind the gag and the sound and feel of knife breaking through bone are what wake him.*

He replayed the dream off and on all night long at the *Gates of Hell*. He didn't court it. It just wouldn't go away. Should Gary have asked him even so much as a *how's it going?* he'd have told him about the dream in an instant in as much detail as he could muster but he didn't ask and Bass couldn't very well blurt it out between banana daiquiris and bijou cocktails.

It was the dream though and dwelling on the dream that goaded him into action the next day.

The Official Gerard Pope Website carried no e-mail address but it did have a message board where readers could discuss his work, swap observations and opinions and Bass noted at first visit that

Gerard tended to log on once a week over the weekend and answer whatever questions had been put to him. He was regular about it.

His style in these messages was encouragingly open and unaffected. He was even funny. Approachable. Bass reflected that though Annabel had forbidden him any contact with her she'd said nothing about Gerard.

Bass sat down, lit a cigarette, took a deep drag and dropped him a line Thursday night after work.

Good photo. She looks great in green. I like the faraway sky-look, of course. Know it well. Care to catch up on old times we never had? If you're curious, e-mail's above.
  —Bass

By Sunday he had a reply.

She'd probably kill me for doing this but yeah, I guess I am curious. You still on the West Side? If so, how about 1:00 Tuesday, lunch at the Aegean?
  —Best, Pope

So he used his last name too. Interesting.

He e-mailed back saying Tuesday was fine.

Monday night he dreamed about something else entirely. At least he thought it was about something else entirely. It was a bright beautiful day and he was driving along a highway when another car pulled up alongside him and Bass and the driver glanced at one another. The driver was a woman, a blonde, slightly overweight he thought, but she gave him a gap-tooth smile that simply beckoned.

The next thing he knew he was in her car, in the passenger seat, and the next thing after *that* they were parked along the roadside and the car had become a trailer and they were naked on her bed making love and even though her body had a fleshy quality it was pretty good, really—not bad at all. It got even better when she morphed into a slim beautiful brunette, the model Paulina Porizkova, who Bass had wanted since he first laid eyes on her. And she kept doing that—morphing from Paulina to the blonde with the gap in her teeth and back again.

"I think maybe you should stay the night," she said as the blonde.

He said, "I thought you'd never ask."

He woke with barely enough time to shower and shave and grab a cup of coffee along the way.

The Aegean was doing a moderate lunch business and there were plenty of open tables but Pope was at the bar at the corner facing the door. He immediately smiled and offered his hand. "Gerard Pope," he said.

"John Bass. How'd you know it was me?"

"What? Oh, the photos."

"Photos?"

"Yeah."

"She kept the photos?"

"Some, I guess. I don't know how many. I just know you from the ones she showed me. Cape May, mostly. You know how it is with the ladies—the ones *she* looked really good in."

He smiled and shook his head. "Damn."

"What'll you have?" said the bartender. Pope was drinking an O'Doul's non-alcoholic.

"Amstel Lite."

"Coming right up."

"I thought she destroyed them all."

"Annabel? Annabel can't throw away a burned-out light bulb."

His beer arrived complete with frosted mug and they asked for menus and talked trivia, about his website for the most part which Bass said he admired and which was handled for him by a fan in Colorado in exchange for collectables, first editions and such and they ordered and then gradually the conversation began to get more personal and Bass learned that they had moved twice in three years into larger better apartments from Hell's Kitchen to the West Side and finally to Soho. He learned two of Pope's books had movie options but that Pope wasn't necessarily counting on anything to come of them. He learned that Annabel was working in mixed-media now, seascapes like stylized beach-combings and that they were selling fairly well out of their Soho loft. They were currently working on a website to promote her stuff too.

By the time he'd finished his broiled squid and calamari salad and Pope his chicken *lemoni* Bass realized something that didn't make him happy at all. He kind of liked the guy. What a pain in the ass. And he guessed that Pope could see it on his face because he laughed.

"Disappointed? That I'm not some prick you could just keep on hating?"

"I never..."

"Come on. If you didn't hate me you were sure working on it. Look, I'm a writer. I'm good at body-language. There was a definite poker up your ass when you walked in. You only just relieved yourself of it a while ago."

He thought of the dream, Gerard's sad nod to him that was almost a bow. He was pretty good at body-language himself. But he only now realized what the nod was telling him. Not resignation to the knife, which was what he'd thought it to be the following morning. *Recognition.* Recognition of the Other.

In his mind he spoke the dream-words *do you love your wife?* but what came out of him was "You love her, don't you."

"Of course I do. She's pretty damn easy to love. Which you of all people ought to know. She was trying to do you a favor, Bass."

"Oh yeah? How so?" He hoped it didn't come out as bitter as it sounded.

"Telling you she'd thrown out the photos, for one thing. Telling you to do the same. By cutting you off. That was the main thing."

Cutting you off. He thought of his dream and suddenly it clarified and almost startled him. He realized that in the subtle inversions dreams will make it hadn't been Gerard sitting tied to the chair at all. *It was Bass.* Unable to move or defend himself, unable to speak or argue his position. Waiting, nodding sadly in recognition of *Gerard.* And finally cut off at the very moment of awakening.

"She knew it wouldn't work. She was trying to do you a kindness by not letting it go any further. And herself a kindness too. Me too of course."

Bass thought about it. Finally he nodded.

"I had a dream about you," he said. "I lit a cigarette. You took it from me and threw it away."

"Pushy little bastard, huh?"

"No. It was for my own damn good."

They split the bill.

"You asked me if I loved my wife," Gerard said—*though he hadn't, exactly.* "If *you* love her you'll do the same as she tried to do for you. Metaphorically at least, throw those damn pictures away. Tear them into little pieces. Maybe someday when we're old and grey, you can take a new one."

"Or maybe not."

"Or maybe not. Nice meeting you, Bass. This never happened but I'm sort of glad it did, if you know what I mean."

Bass ordered another beer and sipped it slowly, thinking things through.

A little while later he switched to scotch.

Midway through the second one he stepped outside for a smoke and watched the street life. Nannies and brisk young mothers with double-wide strollers. Truckers delivering paper goods and dairy. A woman across the street jogging in place at a stoplight and shouting furiously into a cellphone. A guy in a mohawk, moccasins and fur earmuffs, stripped to the waist, all buff and tanned. *What's with that?* he wondered. *Tonto Nuevo?* Earmuffs in August? It seemed there were people out here way more strange and obsessive than he was.

He went back inside and finished his scotch and had another. He sipped this one for a long time. The bartender made no effort to engage him in conversation. Sometimes they just knew.

He paid for the beer and scotches and headed home. Home was as he knew it would be. Empty. Empty of Laura, mostly.

He poured himself a final scotch he certainly didn't need and sat back heavily on the couch and sipped it and he supposed he must have dozed for a little while because the next thing he knew his face was wet with tears, *he was crying in his sleep now for chrissake, that was different* and he thought of the dream and what the dream maybe wanted him to do so he went to the kitchen and opened the drawer and took out the knife.

He looked at the long heavy blade. It needed honing but he guessed it would do the trick. He looked at his fingers spread out on the counter. A symbol, he thought. That was what dreams were all about, weren't they? Symbols for what still needing doing in your life? He lit a cigarette and thought about it some more. *Nah,* he thought. That's more loco than the earmuffs. Not even the tip of a pinkie. You didn't want to take this dream-terminology too damn literally.

Besides, something else had occurred to him. In his dream, the end of his affair with Annabel was loss, pure and simple. Symbolized by a few missing fingers. He thought it was more complex than that.

You lost something, sure. But when you did you added something too.

Scar tissue.

He could live with that.

He put down the knife and stripped off his shirt, pulled deeply on his cigarette and then pressed it slowly to the flesh directly over where he imagined his heart to be. He wanted the burn to last. *Here's to you, Annabel,* he thought. He smelled his chest hair burning and another sweeter smell beneath it and felt something like a hornet's sting, sharp and abrupt and then fading to a bright throb as the ember gutted out.

He tossed the butt into the ashtray and headed for the bacitracin.

Roughly seven years later preparatory to Annabel and Gerard's tenth anniversary party he stepped out of a steaming shower and admired the pale white circle that stood out plainly against his glowing flesh.

Laura was already waiting, dressed and ready to go.

She always was a bit ahead of him.

About a year or so before I wrote this I'd had a deeply painful breakup and like my character here felt utterly shut out of this woman's life and utterly adrift. Worse so when I learned she'd married. But like Annabel in the story she was ultimately wiser than I. And over time I became reconciled to that fact—though the meeting with her husband is wholly fictional.

The wedding photo I refer to is actually a photo of my friends Gerard Houarner and Linda Addison, who wed at Mardi Gras.

Many happy returns of many happy days.

—JK

At Home with the VCR

"Jeez. *Now* what are you watching?"

"Early Cronenberg. *Rabid*. Great movie. C'mere. Sit your butt down next to me on the couch here."

"Oh god. Is this another one of your godawful horror movies?"

"Uh-huh. But this one's a classic. Come on. Sit down."

"What's that *thing* coming out of her armpit? Oh god. It looks like a..."

"Hypodermic dick. *Penis dentata*. Yeah, I know. See, she's had major cosmetic surgery because of this burn accident and..."

"Isn't that Marilyn Chambers?"

"Uh-huh. Her first non-porn role. Looks great, doesn't she? Surprise is, she can act. She's good."

"God, this is *disgusting.* Can't you turn it down?"

"It's a *horror movie*, Susan. You can't *turn it down*."

TIME PASSES.

"She does have a wonderful body."

"You got *that* right. Damn!"

"I bet she works out. She definitely works out. What year was this movie?"

" '76, '77. Something like that."

"Hardly anybody was working out then. I mean, it wasn't a *thing* like it is now."

"Marilyn was a-*head* of her time."

"Wiseass!"

"Ow!"

TIME PASSES.

"Oh, gross! I don't see how you can watch this stuff."

"Shhhh."

"I'm getting myself a beer. You want a beer? Hey, you want a beer or not?"

TIME PASSES.

MORE TIME PASSES.

"Actually, I felt kinda sorry for her. I mean there at the end."

"Sure. You were supposed to. Wasn't her fault. Like the Frankenstein monster. Wasn't his fault either. Hit the OFF button, will you?"

"You were right I guess. It wasn't bad. For a horror movie. Got me pretty nervous there."

"That's not all it got you."

"Huh?"

"How long have I known you, Susan?"

"Two years in July. You know that."

"Right. And you don't think I know the look on your face when something turns you on? After *two years*?"

"It didn't *turn me on*, for godsakes! It was a *horror* movie."

"I'll make you a bet. I'll bet you five bucks that if I touch you right now, you're wet."

"Right. Sure. Wet. Of course."

"You gonna take the bet?"

"No I will not *take the bet*."

"Why not?"

"Because."

"Why not?"

"Stop it, Richard, come *on*, stop it! That *tickles*! Richard! *Stop it! Stop...*"

TIME PASSES.

"Mmmmm. That's nice. That's *really* nice. Do that some more, okay?"

"Give me my five bucks first."

"Later. Right now just do that some more, okay? No, wait. Hold it. I got an idea. Rewind. Go to that part in the movie theatre. You know? You know the part I mean? Where the guy has his hand up inside her shirt, right before the thing bites him or injects him or whatever and...yeah...that's right...that part there, where he's just starting to...that's right...now hit the SLOW button...now come here and yes, yes... *mmmmmmmmmmm...* that's so *nice...*"

In 1999 my friend Dean Kaltsas was running the first-ever Erotica USA Festival here in New York City at the Jacob Javits Center. He asked me if I'd like to be a guest and write a little something for their souvenir program magazine.

Would I like to be a guest?

An entire immense hall filled with half-naked women? Demonstrating the use of various sex toys?

Does *Ursus Arctos* deposit the occasional scat in heavily foliated localities?

Talk about a no-brainer.

I was the only honor-writer in attendance there so I decided that my piece for the magazine would combine the sexual with the spooky. Cronenberg's *Rabid* is one of my favorites and one of his sexiest—not to mention Marilyn Chambers' finest hour unless you count *Insatiable* which on reflection I guess I do—so it seemed a natural place to proceed from.

The very simple dialogue structure was fun too.

—JK

Those Rockports Won't Get You into Heaven

The place was going all to hell—not that you'd necessarily notice unless you worked there. The floor was mopped and the glasses fairly clean. The bottles were dusted and the bar wiped down but then I took care of that.

But the owner had two other restaurants on the same block and kept swapping bottles back and forth between them. So you never knew when you came in after the day shift what would be on the shelves. You'd have plenty of Dewars one day and the next day maybe a quarter of a bottle. It also meant that you'd find a liter of peach brandy or port wine getting overly chummy with the single-malts. The wines kept changing according to whoever threw him the best deal that week and half the time there was no beer on tap whatsoever.

Waiters, busboys, hostesses—everybody was owed back pay. Myself included half the time.

It was March and one of the coldest longest goddamn winters on record and the heat was off again. Had been all week. All we had between us and runny noses was a single space-heater looking lonely and pathetic behind the hostess' station. Customers ate their *taramasalata* and *souvlakia* with their coats on.

There weren't many of them. You don't associate *Greek cuisine* with frozen tundra.

It was six o'clock Thursday evening and of my dwindling group of regulars not a single one had show up. I couldn't blame them. They were all wised up to the heating situation. We had more waiters and busboys than customers. Two couples and a party of four in the restaurant and that was that.

I was going fucking broke here.

Not a tip on the bar in two hours.

I polished bottles. It's a bartender thing. You got nothing to do you polish bottles.

When the guy walked in with his kid trailing along behind him the first thing I thought was Westchester. Either that or Connecticut. I don't know why because plenty of guys around here are partial to Ralph Lauren and Rockports and outfit their kids in L.L. Bean. But there was something vaguely displaced about him. That's the best I can do. He didn't belong here.

You get so you kind of sense this shit.

They walked directly to the bar but neither one sat down. The kid maybe fourteen I guessed and taking his cue from dad.

"Glass of white wine," he said.

"Sure. We've got pinot grigio, chardonnay, and two Greek wines—Santorini and Kouros. Both very nice. What can I get for you?"

"Whatever."

"Would you care to taste one?"

"No, that's okay. Give me the Santorini."

"You got it."

Like I say you just get a sense about these things. The guy was *wrong* somehow. Wound so fucking tight he was practically ready to give off sparks should he start to do any *un*winding and you probably didn't want to see that.

You're not supposed to have an underage kid with you at a bar in New York City but most of the time we look the other way and most of the time the guy will order his kid a Coke or something and we look the other way on that too. This guy didn't. And of course I didn't offer.

I poured the wine and he drained off half of it in one swallow.

"I used to come in here all the time," he said. Not to me but to his kid.

Though he wasn't *looking* at his kid.

His eyes were all over the place. The rows of bottles behind me, the murals on the wall, the ceiling, the tables and chairs in the restaurant. But I had the feeling he wasn't really seeing much of it. Like he was scanning but not exactly *tracking*. Except when he turned to look out the plate-glass windows to the street beyond.

That seemed to focus him. He drank some more.

"It's changed hands, hell, maybe a dozen times since then. This was way before I met your mother."

The kid was looking at him. He still wasn't looking back. Or at me either for that matter. He kept scanning. As though he were expecting something to jump out of the clay amphorae or the floral arrangements. That and turning back to the window and the street.

"Not really, sir," I said. "You must be thinking of another place. A lot of turnaround on the Avenue but not here. It's been the Santorini for about ten years now and before that it was a Mexican restaurant, Sombrero, from about the mid-fifties on. So unless you're a whole lot older than you look..."

"Really?"

"That's right."

"Damn. I could have sworn..."

He was trying to act as cool and casual as the clothes he had on but I could feel him flash and burn suddenly all the same. He didn't like me correcting him in front of his kid. Tough shit, I thought. Fuck you. Snap judgments are part of my stock in trade and I hadn't liked him from the minute he walked in. He made an attempt at a save.

"I used to live around here. Long time ago. Early seventies."

"Really? Where was that?"

"Seventy-first, just off the park."

"Nice over there. And pretty pricey these days. So where are you folks now?"

"We're out in Rye."

Westchester, I thought. Gotcha.

He turned back to the street again. I noticed that his son was staring at me and I thought, jesus, if this guy looked displaced his kid looked absolutely *lost.* He had big brown eyes as bright and clear as a doe's eyes and the eyes seemed to want to make contact with me. For just a second there I let them.

It could have just been me but it felt like he was looking as me as though I were some kind of crazy lifeline. It wasn't a look I was used to. Not after two divorces and fifteen years bartending.

"I'll have another," the guy said.

I poured it for him and watched him gulp it down.

"We don't get over this way much anymore," he said. "Hardly at all. His mother's across the street shopping."

His mother, I thought. Not my wife but his mother. That was interesting.

And I figured I had it now—pretty much all of a piece. What I had here in front of me was one stone alky sneaking a couple of nervous quick ones while the little wife wasn't looking. Dragging his kid into a bar while she was out spending all that hard-earned money he was probably making by managing *other* people's hard-earned money so he could afford the house in Rye, the Rockports and the Ralph Lauren and L.L. Bean.

I wondered exactly where she was spending it. Betsy Johnson, Intermix and Lucky Brand Dungarees I figured would be way too young for anybody he'd be married to and I doubted she'd be bothering with the plates and soaps or scented candles over at Details. That left either L'Occitane if she was into perfume or Hummel Jewelers.

My bet was on the jewelers.

My other bet was that there was great big trouble in paradise.

And I was thinking this when I heard the *pop pop pop* from down the street.

The kid heard it too.

"What was that?" he said. He turned to the windows.

The guy shrugged and drained his wine. "Backfire, probably. I'll have one more, thanks." He set the glass down.

Only it wasn't backfire. I knew that right away.

When my first wife Helen and I lived in New Jersey we'd now and then get slightly loaded afternoons and take her little Colt Pony and my .22 rimfire semiauto out to the fields behind our house and plunk some cans and bottles. The Colt made pretty much the same sound.

Ordinarily I'd have been out in the street by now.

Instead I poured him the wine.

This time the guy sipped slowly. Seemed calmer all of a sudden. I revised my thinking bigtime about him being just another alky. His eyes stopped skittering over the walls and settled on the bar in front of him.

"Dad?" the kid said.

"Uh-huh."

"Shouldn't we go see how mom's doing?"

"She's shopping. She's doing fine. She loves shopping."

"Yeah, but..."

And now it was the kid's eyes that were darting all over the place.

"We don't want to rush her, do we. I'll just finish my wine here. Then we'll go see what she's up to."

I got that look from the kid again. The look seemed to say *do something, say something* and I considered it for a moment.

The phone on the wall decided for me.

By the time I finished noting down the take-out order—Greek salad, mixed cold appetizers, calamari, roasted quail and two cans of *Sprite* for godsakes—the woman's name, address and phone number, the guy was reaching for his wallet. His hands were shaking. His face was flushed.

"What's the damage?"

"That's twenty-four dollars, sir."

He fished out a ten and a twenty and downed the last of his wine.

"Keep the change," he said.

Nice tip, I thought. You don't see twenty-five per cent much. Maybe the bar at the Plaza but not in this place. I figured he wanted me to remember him.

I figured I would remember him. Vividly.

The kid turned back to look at me once as he followed his father out the door. It was possible that I might have seen a flash of anger or maybe a kind of panic there but I could have been imagining that. You couldn't be sure.

I rang up the wine and cleared his glass and wiped down the bar. He'd spilled a little.

There were a few ways to play this. First I could be straight about it and report exactly what I saw. All of what I saw. Not just his being there but the high-wire tension going slack as shoestrings once the shots went off and then all nervous again when he was about to leave. The way the kid kept looking at me. Or just for fun I could try to fuck the guy over royally and completely by saying gee, I really didn't remember him at all to tell the truth. Though that might not work if his kid said otherwise. Finally I could find out who he was and shake him down for a whole lot more than twenty-five per-cent in maybe a day or so.

Hell, I already knew where he lived.

But I pretty much knew what I was going to do.

As I say, I've had two divorces and know what a bitch they can be. And I'm no big fan of married women in general either.

But my daughter by my second wife was just about this kid's age. Maybe a bit younger.

I wondered who he'd hired. How much he'd paid. If they'd actually hit the jewelry store just for show or only the woman inside it.

I polished bottles—it's a bartender thing—and waited for the gawkers and the sirens and New York's finest to come on in.

Thanks to Matt Long

I was sitting in my local bar at cocktail hour one day when this guy walked in with his kid and started exactly this kind of conversation with the bartender, Matt Long. The guy was skittish and nervous as a colt and Matt and I talked about it later. We decided that probably dad had visitation rights and that he was new at this father-and-son minus mom bit.

Then I got a darker notion.

—JK

Olivia: A Monologue

Olivia and I met at State University, organizing Women's Week. She sort of scared me at first. She was still living with her boyfriend yet here she is looking at me in this certain way. I'd known I was gay since the eleventh grade and by then I thought I was smart enough not to get involved with some curious straight woman with a boyfriend. Sure I was. Because when she put her hand on my leg in the Caféteria I let it stay there. And when she kissed me that night I kissed her back. She had a way of looking at you like she was looking straight down into your soul and god, she was beautiful. Her mother was Puerto Rican, her father Iranian-American. To a Manhattan Jewish girl like me she was I guess you'd say exotic. When she broke up with her boyfriend it was like I finally had permission to fall in love with her. And I did. I did love her.

We used to go camping. It was one of those things we liked to do. She called me an amateur because I always wanted to build a fire while she had this little butane camp stove. So there I am with my hot dog on a stick and cans of beans and sauerkraut sitting in the embers while she's next to me making scampi.

Anyhow we were in Pennsylvania that day, on the Appalachian Trail and there was nobody at the campground but us. I get up in the morning and walk over to the public restroom and we thought we were alone out there so I was naked and I get halfway down the trail and there's this guy coming out of the woods and he's weird looking. Pale, knit cap in the middle of summer, sweatpants, ratty tee-shirt. Got a cigarette? he asks me. And he's laughing. Because how would I have a cigarette. I'm naked! And I said jeez my god! I'm sorry and I'm so embarrassed I could die. So I run back to the tent, to Olivia and tell her we've got to get dressed, there's a man out here.

We decided to move to another campground. We pack our gear and start walking and just beyond the first bend in the trail there's this guy again and he says see you later and I said, see you later, not meaning anything, just something you say and then in a while we stop to check the map and there he is coming along behind us a little ways downtrail and this time he catches us laughing, kissing. So there I am embarrassed twice in one day and now he's got this rifle against his hip though it's not hunting season and he says, you lost? We're fine, Olivia told him. Okay, see you later he says and this time I don't say anything, I just watch him walk away and disappear.

I figured we'd lost him. There were lots of campsites around and we didn't see him after that so we found a spot and settled in. Had dinner, went to bed. And we were making love. Inside the tent. And I remember Olivia's hands on me, I can remember the feel of them to this day. And that was when my arm just exploded.

I took five shots. Arm-neck-neck-face-head. If my mouth hadn't been closed my molars wouldn't have shattered the bullet to my face and I'd be dead. They told me if I'd been turned a centimeter to the left the third shot would have gone directly through my jugular. Olivia took two, in the back and in the head. I pulled her behind a tree and I'm thinking I've got to go get help or we'll both bleed to death and she's saying no, don't go, please don't, like she wants us to die together, die in one another's arms and then she's trying to put her shoes on like she'll go too, we'll both get out of there together but she couldn't, she couldn't stand up, she kept falling.

I watched her die.

Right before she died she went blind. She couldn't see. She told me to take her wallet out of her shirt pocket, said you'll need money and in the tiniest little voice she said, go. But I couldn't go. I loved her. I knew what was happening. I just watched her.

They caught him. He'd left a trail of cigarette butts and Coke cans and his prints were all over them and it turned out he'd done this before, it wasn't the first time. They asked him why. Because we were lesbians he said. Dykes. Because he saw us kissing. Because he couldn't stand to see that.

Two people. In love.

Thanks to Chris Golden

Some years ago I decided it would be fun to try my hand at directing for theatre again, which I hadn't done since the seventies. My friend Theo Levine was fond of the one-man-show concept and I directed him in two of them, one of which was called *Sereal*—a series of monologues he'd written from the first-person point of view of serial killers such as Dahmer, Manson, Eileen Wournos, Ed Gein—a whole nasty bunch of 'em. Some of it was dark comedy and some of it was deadly serious. We found ourselves a black-box midtown theatre and I helped him with the rewrites and we started rehearsing.

Somewhere along the way we decided it would be a neat idea to enlist the aid of an actress who would do no speaking, just movement. A kind of silent Greek chorus who would also occasionally dip into the action to get strangled, stabbed or whatever.

Then at some point along the way I started feeling we were missing something.

The victim's point of view.

It wasn't there. Mime-stabbings just weren't...cutting it.

For a while I'd been sitting on a news clipping that Christopher Golden had sent me, saying he thought it had the makings of a Ketchum story. I dug it out and based very closely on that wrote the only piece in the play that wasn't Theo's and we gave it to our actress—who was thrilled to be doing a real character for a change— as a single monologue which would end the play in which she'd been so noticeably silent throughout. The last word would be the victim's.

It worked. So well in fact that I decided to use Olivia's basic story again as the opening murder-scene in *The Lost*.

The monologue itself had never been published, though. So when Monica O'Rourke asked me for a short piece for the 2005 World Horror Convention Magazine I gladly handed it over.

—JK

Brave Girl

"Police Operator 321. Where's your emergency?"
     "It's my mommy."
The voice on the other end was so small that even its sex was indeterminate. The usual questions were not going to apply.

"What happened to your mommy?"
"She fell."
"Where did she fall?"
"In the bathroom. In the tub."
"Is she awake?"
"Unh-unh."
"Is there water in the tub?"
"I made it go away."
"You drained the tub?"
"Uh-huh."
"Good. Okay. My name is Officer Price. What's yours?"
"Suzy."
"Is there anybody else in the house, Suzy?"
"Unh-unh."
"Okay, Suzy. I want you to stay on the line, okay? Don't hang up. I'm going to transfer you to Emergency Services and they're going to help you and your mommy, all right? Don't hang up now, okay?"
"Okay."
He punched in EMS.
"Dana, it's Tom. I've got a little girl, can't be more than four or five. Name's Suzy. She says her mother's unconscious. Fell in the bathroom."
"Got it."

It was barely ten o'clock and shaping up to be a busy summer day. Electrical fire at Knott's Hardware over on Elm and Main just under an hour ago. Earlier, a three-car pile-up on route 6—somebody hurrying to get to work through a deceptive sudden pocket of Maine fog. A heart-attack at Bel Haven Rest Home only minutes after that. The little girl's address was up on the computer screen. 415 Whiting Road. Listing under the name L. Jackson.

"Suzy?"

"Uh-huh."

"This is Officer Keeley, Suzy. I want you to stand by a moment, all right? I'm not going to put you on hold. Just stay on the phone. Sam? You with me?"

"Yup."

"Okay, Suzy. Your mommy fell, right? In the bathroom?"

"Yeah."

"And she's unconscious?"

"Huh?"

"She's not awake?"

"Unh-uhn."

"Can you tell if she's breathing?"

"I...I think."

"We're on it," said Sam.

"Is your front door unlocked, Suzy?"

"The door?"

"Your front door."

"I don't know."

"Do you know how to lock and unlock the front door, Suzy?"

"Yes. Mommy showed me."

"Okay. I want you to put the phone down somewhere—don't hang up but just put it down somewhere, okay? and go see if the door's unlocked. And if it isn't unlocked, I want you to unlock it so that we can come in and help mommy, okay? But don't hang up the phone, all right? Promise?"

"Promise."

She heard a rattling sound. Telephone against wood.

Excellent.

In a moment she heard the girl pick up again.

"Hi."

"Did you unlock the door, Suzy?"

"Uh-huh. It was locked."

"But you unlocked it."

"Uh-huh."

I love this kid, she thought. *This kid is terrific.*

"Great, Suzy. You're doing absolutely great. We'll be over there in a couple of minutes, okay? Just a few minutes now. Did you see what happened to your mommy? Did you see her fall?"

"I was in my bedroom. I heard a big thump."

"So you don't know why she fell?

"Unh-unh. She just did."

"Did she ever fall before, Suzy?"

"Unh-unh."

"Does mommy take any medicine?"

"Huh?"

"Does mommy take any medicine? Has she been sick at all?"

"She takes aspirin sometimes."

"Just aspirin?"

"Uh-huh."

"How old are you, Suzy?"

"Four."

"Four? Wow, that's pretty old!"

Giggles. "Is not."

"Listen, mommy's going to be just fine. We're on our way and we're going to take good care of her. You're not scared or anything, are you?"

"Nope."

"Good girl. 'Cause you don't need to be. Everything's going to be fine."

"Okay."

"Do you have any relatives who live nearby, Suzy? Maybe an aunt or an uncle? Somebody we can call to come and stay with you for a while, while we take care of mommy?"

"Grandma. Grandma stays with me."

"Okay, who's grandma? Can you give me her name?"

Giggles again. "Grandma, silly."

She heard sirens in the background. *Good response time,* she thought. *Not bad at all.*

"Okay, Suzy. In a few minutes the police are going to come to your door..."

"I can see them through the window!"

She had to smile at the excitement in her voice.

"Good. And they're going to ask you a lot of the same questions I just asked you. Okay?"

"Yes."

"You tell them just what you told me."

"Okay."

"And then there are going to be other people, they'll be dressed all in white, and they're going to come to the door in a few minutes. They'll bring mommy to the hospital so that a doctor can see her and make sure she's all better. All right?"

"Yes."

She heard voices, footfalls, a door closing. A feminine voice asking the little girl for the phone.

"'Bye."

"Bye, Suzy. You did really, really *good.*"

"Thanks."

And she had.

"Minty, badge 457. We're on the scene."

She told Minty about the grandmother and when it was over Officer Dana Keeley took a very deep breath and smiled. This was one to remember. A four-year-old kid who very likely just saved her mother from drowning. She'd check in with the hospital later to see about the condition of one L. Jackson but she felt morally certain they were in pretty good shape here. In the meantime she couldn't wait to tell Chuck. She knew her husband was going to be proud of her. Hell, she was proud of her. She thought she'd set just the right tone with the little girl—friendly and easy—plus she'd got the job done down to the last detail.

The girl hadn't even seemed terribly frightened.

That was the way it was supposed to go of course, she was there to keep things calm among other things but still it struck her as pretty amazing.

Four years old. Little Suzy, she thought, was quite a child. She hoped that when the time came for her and Chuck they'd have the parenting skills and the sheer good luck to have kids who turned out as well as she did.

She wondered if the story'd make the evening news. She thought it deserved a mention.

"Incredible," Minty said. "Little girl's all of four years old.

She knows enough to dial 911, gives the dispatcher everything she needs, has the good sense to turn off the tap and hit the drain lever so her mother doesn't drown, knows exactly where her mother's address book is so we can locate Mrs. Jackson over there, shows us up to the bathroom where mom's lying naked, with blood all over the place for godsakes..."

"I know," said Crocker. "I wanna be just like her when I grow up."

Minty laughed but it might easily have been no laughing matter. Apparently Liza Jackson had begun to draw her morning bath and when she stepped into the still-flowing water, slipped and fell, because when they found her she had one dry leg draped over the ledge of the tub and the other buckled under her. She'd hit the ceramic soap dish with sufficient force to splatter blood from her head-wound all the way up to the shower rod.

Hell of a thing for a little kid to see.

Odd that she hadn't mentioned all that blood to the dispatcher. Head-wounds—even ones like Liza Jackson's which didn't seem terribly serious—bled like crazy. For a four-year-old she'd imagine it would be pretty scary. But then she hadn't had a problem watching the EMS crew wheel her barely-conscious mother out into the ambulance either. This was one tough-minded little girl.

"What did you get from the grandmother?"

"She didn't want to say a whole lot in front of the girl but I gather the divorce wasn't pretty. He's moved all the way out to California, sends child support when he gets around to it. Liza Jackson's living on inherited money from the grandfather and a part-time salary at, uh, let's see..."

He flipped through his pad, checked his notes.

"...a place called It's the Berries..."

"I know it. Country store kind of affair, caters to the tourist trade. Does most of its business during summer and leaf-season. Dried flower arrangements, potpourri, soaps and candles, jams and honey. That kind of thing."

"She's got no brothers or sisters. But Mrs. Jackson has no problem with taking care of Suzy for the duration."

"Fine."

She glanced at them over on the sofa. Mrs. Jackson was smiling slightly, brushing out the girl's long straight honey-brown hair. A *hospital's no place for a little girl*, she'd said. *We'll wait for word here.* The EMS crew had assured them that while, yes, there was the possibility of concussion and concussions could be tricky, she'd come around very quickly, so that they doubted the head-wound was serious, her major problem at this point being loss of blood—and Mrs. Jackson was apparently willing to take them at their word. Minty wouldn't have, had it been her daughter. But then Minty wasn't a Maine-iac born and bred and tough as a rail spike. Suzy had her back to the woman, her expression unreadable—a pretty, serious-looking little girl in a short blue-and-white checkered dress that was not quite a party dress but not quite the thing for pre-school either.

When they'd arrived she'd still been in her pajamas. She guessed the dress was grandma's idea.

The press would like it. There was a local tv crew waiting outside—waiting patiently for a change. The grandmother had already okayed the interview.

They were pretty much squared away here.

She walked over to the couch.

"Do you need us to stay, Mrs. Jackson? Until the interview's through I mean."

"That's not necessary, Officer. We can handle this ourselves, I'm sure."

She stood and extended her hand. Minty took it. The woman's grip was firm and dry.

"I want to thank you for your efforts on my daughter's behalf," she said. "And for arriving as promptly as you did."

"Thank you, ma'am. But the one we've all got to thank, really, is your granddaughter. Suzy? You take good care now, okay?"

"I will."

Minty believed her.

Carole Belliver had rarely done an interview that went so smoothly. The little girl had no timidity whatsoever in front of the camera—she didn't fidget, she didn't stutter, she didn't weave back and forth or shift out of frame—all of which was typical behavior for adults on camera. She answered Carole's questions clearly and without hesitation. Plus she was pretty as all hell. The camera loved her.

There was only one moment of unusable tape because of something the girl had done as opposed to their usual false stops and starts and that was when she dropped the little blonde doll she was holding and stooped to pick it up and the dress she was wearing was so short you could see her white panties which Carole glimpsed briefly and promptly glanced away from, and then wondered why. Was it that the little girl acted and sounded so much like a miniature adult that Carole was embarrassed for her, as you would be for an adult?

It was possible. She'd done and thought sillier things in her life.

The piece was fluff of course but it was *good* fluff. Not some flower-show or county fair but a real human interest story for a change. Unusual and touching. With a charming kid as its heroine. She could be proud of this one. This one wasn't going to make her cringe when it was broadcast.

It occurred to her that they could all be proud of this one, everybody involved really, from the dispatchers god knows to the police and EMS team to the grandmother who'd no doubt helped raise this little wonder and finally, extending even to her and her crew. Everybody got to do their job, fulfill their responsibilities efficiently and well. And the one who had made all of this happen for them was a four-year-old.

Quite a day.

They had down all the reactions shots. All they needed now was her tag line.

"This is Carole Bellaver—reporting to you on a brave, exceptional little girl—from Knottsville, Maine."

"Got it," Bernie said.

"You want to cover it?"

"Why? *I said I got it.*"

"Okay. Jeez, fine."

What the hell was *that* about? *Bernie had just snapped at her.* Bernie was the nicest, most easygoing cameraman she'd ever worked with. She couldn't believe it. It was totally out of character.

He and Harold, her soundman, were packing their gear into the van as if they were in some big hurry to get out of there. And she realized now that they'd both been unusually silent ever since the interview. Normally when the camera stopped rolling you couldn't shut them up.

But the interview had gone well. *Hadn't it?*

Was it something she'd said or done?

By now the print media had arrived, some of them all the way from Bangor and Portland and they were talking to Suzy and her grandmother on the front steps where she'd taped them earlier. Flashbulbs popped. Suzy smiled.

Bernie and Harold looked grim.

"Uh, guys. You want to let me into the loop? I thought everything went fine here."

"It did," Bernie said.

"So? So what's the problem?"

"You didn't see? You were standing right there. I thought you must have—then went on anyway. Sorry."

"See what?"

"When she dropped the doll."

"Right, I saw her drop the doll."

"And she bent down to pick it up."

"Yeah?"

He sighed. "I've got it all on tape. We can take a look over at the studio. I want to know it wasn't just my imagination."

"It wasn't," Harold said. "I saw it too."

"I don't get it. What are you talking about?"

She glanced over at Suzy on the steps. The girl was looking directly at her, ignoring the reporters, frowning—and for a moment held her gaze. *She's sick of this*, Carole thought. *That's the reason for the frown.* She smiled. Suzy didn't.

And she had no idea what all the mystery was about until they rolled the tape at the studio and she watched the little girl drop the doll and stoop and Bernie said *there* and stopped the tape so that she saw what she hadn't noticed at the time because she'd looked away so abruptly, strangely embarrassed for this little girl so mature and adult for her age so that they'd simply not registered for her—the long wide angry welts along the back of both thighs just below the pantyline which told her that this was not only a smart, brave little girl but perhaps a sad and foolish one too who had drained the tub dry and dialed 911 to save her mother's life.

Which may not have been worth saving.

Nobody had noticed this. Not the cops, not EMS. Nobody.

She rolled the tape again. Jesus.

She wondered about the grandmother. She *had* to know. How could she not know?

"What do you want to do?" Bernie said.

She felt a kind of hardness, an access to stone will.

Not unlike the little girl's perhaps. She remembered that last look from the steps.

"I want to phone the reporters who were out there with us, kill the story. Dupe the tapes. Phone the police and child welfare and get copies to them. I want us to do what her daughter evidently couldn't bring herself to do. I want us to do our best to drown the bitch."

They both seemed fine with that.

I heard an item on CNN one night about a four-year-old girl who'd saved her mother's life because her parents had the forethought to teach her to dial 911 in an emergency. Which I thought extremely smart of them and pretty extraordinary on the little girl's part. One of the really *good* stories about people you rarely ever hear on the news.

So then of course I had to turn it nasty.

—JK

Honor System

It was the rabbit that did it.

She'd been driving for hours, stressed-out pretty much all the way up 1-75 from her apartment in Naples to her brother's condo in Sarasota—*and just because her brother wouldn't answer his phone*—when instead of going that far north she could have knocked two hours off her travel time and all that driving in the dark along lonely, two-lane State Road 70 by switching to 17 and cutting right on over to Arcadia, the only goddamn town along all this long, awful stretch of highway if you could even call it a highway, the town twenty, maybe twenty-five miles behind her now finally and already feeling like a distant memory.

But no. Joel wasn't answering his phone. So instead it had been well over an hour and a half on 70 even to get this far, with thick bands of low-lying fog at every dip of the road, so that driving was like diving and surfacing through waves just about to break along the shoreline, diving and surfacing over and over again, her wipers at maximum speed barely up to the job.

Were it not for Joel she could have been there already.

But she had no choice. She had to tell him somehow.

Their uncle was in Lawnwood Regional at Ft. Pierce. He'd been pulling out of a Wal-Mart parking lot when a couple of kids out joyriding came careening around a corner and rammed his car nearly head-on. Despite the belt and harness his head had hit the driver's-side window hard enough to crack it. Now he was in a coma. His doctors were monitoring him very carefully.

Linda and Joel had spent every summer with Ed and Marion Teale from the seventh grade on, all the way through high-school, their aunt and uncle the sole safe haven from their warring parents for six of the most emotionally precarious years of their lives. If you added that up it came to an entire year and a half. A year and a half of sanity and unconditional love in the mountains, woods and lakes of rural New Jersey. It had made all the difference in the world.

Linda met her first boyfriend there, unexpected and delightful as a light summer rain. Childless themselves but infinitely understanding, Uncle Ed and Aunt Marion welcomed the relationship. Her father never would have.

Joel had grown from a fat awkward kid to a reasonably good-looking and reasonably self-possessed young man.

And now Ed might be dying. Her aunt's voice on the phone made that clear. All the brightness leeched away.

There was no way in hell she wasn't going see him before that happened. If only to tell him once again how much he'd meant to her, how much she'd always loved him. Coma or no coma.

Joel was of another mind.

"There's nothing we can do, Lin. Hell, I love the guy too, you know that. But I can't go through this again. It's been what? eight months since mom died? A year and a half since dad? I just can't take another hospital right now."

"It's Alice, isn't it. You look like hell, Joel."

"Thanks a lot."

"Well, you do."

The wrinkled U Mass sweatshirt didn't hide much. He was a good ten pounds below his fighting weight. Maybe more like twenty.

"Look. When Jim left me all I wanted to do was climb under the covers and sleep the rest of my life away. I know exactly how you feel. Instead I set the clock, even on Sunday. You going to the office?"

"Of course I'm going to the office."

"Good. But you've got to get the rest of your priorities straight too, Joel. Clean up around here for godsakes. Do a laundry. Answer your goddamn phone or at least turn on the machine. Remember these?"

She held out her left wrist. The faint white scars were horizontal.

The hospital psychologist had called them a cry for help, not a serious attempt at suicide.

"I'm not even sure I'd be here without those two people in my life. Are you? Are you really sure? You want to find me, you know where I'll be."

And picturing him standing there so lost and alone in the doorway she could almost cry again. But she wouldn't. Not with those headlights coming at her over the hill. Not with the fog whipping at her windshield. Not with the black empty road behind her and the black empty road ahead. She dipped her brights and the oncoming car did the same.

Not a car. A truck.

A semi on this narrow lane doing seventy-five at least for god's sake when they only gave you sixty, so that the little Nissan felt sucked into the vacuum of its wake, shuddering as though somebody had walked over its grave. She flicked on the brights again.

And that was when the dog ran out in front of her.

Dog or wolf—they had them here—something gray in the fog loping across the road maybe three car-lengths ahead so that she instinctively tapped the brake but there was no need, thank god, not really, three car-lengths was far enough away. The dog or whatever it was had disappeared. It was never really in any danger.

It was just that there was so damn much road-kill out here.

She'd been highly aware of it all along, even before Arcadia. But it had gotten much worse now that she was headed toward Lake Okeechobee. It seemed to her that every half mile or so her brights would race across another carcass, pale against the even paler February frost along the roadside to her left or right and sometimes both together as though they'd somehow died in pairs.

Didn't anybody ever clean up around here?

Or was this the fruit of a single day?

It seemed impossible. That so much life could end so violently along one road in the course of just one day. She'd been able to make out the bodies of dogs, skunks, birds, a cat, at least two raccoons, even a huge turtle—and once, lying in the middle of the road across the center line so that both she and the car coming toward her had to brake and slow to a crawl to avoid it, a deer, impossible to tell whether it was male or female, its head little more than a dark pulp glistening in her headlights. She'd had to look away.

They'd made her nervous from the start, all these bodies.

The dog made her more so.

So that the natural impulse was to go faster. To just get the hell out of here as fast as possible. She knew she had to restrain herself from doing that. Doing that could get her killed. Suppose another deer came along? Suppose another deer came along and she had to swerve *just as another truck bore down on her?*

But the tension of *not* slowing down was making her nuts. That and all the rest. Her fatigue, Joel, the late hour, the lonely road, the oncoming headlights—*would they even dim this time?*—her aunt and uncle, the carcasses. All of it. She didn't even dare to light a cigarette. She wanted it over with. She wanted to be somewhere warm and safe and fucking well-lit for a change. She wanted *not* to want to cry.

But it was the rabbit that did it.

The jackrabbit leaping out in front of her in a zigzag line across the road and not three car-lengths away this time but simply *there* in her lights like a sudden ghost image of itself so that she had to slam hard on the brakes, the harness cutting across her chest, something burning *inside* her chest in that terrible moment of expectation, the implicit impact of living flesh on cold unyielding steel.

Which mercifully never came.

Her heart was hammering anyhow. She couldn't believe she'd missed it.

She slowed to fifty-five and forced her hands to relax their grip on the wheel.

She felt queasy and light-headed, as though she hadn't eaten. The half-finished ham and Swiss sandwich in the clear Ziploc bag on the passenger seat was proof that she had. But she was definitely, seriously shaky now... What was the saying? *Three's the charm?*

If this happened to her a third time she'd end up in a ditch.

To her left, another dead cat.

Further on, something wholly unrecognizable but for patchy tufts of fur stirring as she passed.

She glanced down at the speedometer. Sixty-eight, heading toward seventy. *Not good.* She hadn't been aware of speeding up at all. Yet another wave of fog broke over the windshield. For a moment she could see nothing whatsoever ahead or on either side.

So that when the What-U-Need Motel *vacancy* sign appeared ahead she knew she could not do another two hours of this shit, no way, not tonight, it was already nearly midnight so she was not going to get to see her uncle tonight anyway, so she pulled off the road onto the gravel driveway—and by simply doing so felt a weight lift off of her. She actually smiled for the first time in what must have been hours. *What-U-Need? What I need is a goddamn cigarette,* she thought.

In her headlights she saw that the motel consisted of no more than a dozen or so small dark wooden cabins standing in a half-circle on either side of a brightly lit reception office. That was different. More what you'd expect to find in New England than in Florida, where the usual setup was at least twice as many squat concrete units linked on either side around the barely used yet for some reason obligatory pool.

Vacancy seemed to be an understatement. There wasn't another car in sight.

She parked and got out of the Nissan and even before she opened the office door had a feeling of *emptiness* about the place and saw that there was nobody at the desk. She hoped this wasn't going to be a problem. Midnight wasn't all *that* late, was it? Inside she saw that there was no registry book in evidence nor any bell or buzzer to summon clerk or owner either. And then she read the sign over the old antique cash register directly in front of her.

WELCOME TO THE WHAT-U-NEED MOTEL
WE OPERATE *STRICTLY* ON THE HONOR SYSTEM!
RATES, $15.00 PER NIGHT SINGLE, $30.00 PER
NIGHT DOUBLE
CHECK-OUT TIME, 11:00 A.M.
KEYS TO YOUR LEFT, BAR IN BACK!
ALL DRINKS $2.00, SOFT DRINKS ON THE HOUSE!
TAKE WHAT-U-NEED
AND RING IT UP IN THE MORNING
HAVE A GOOD STAY!

Honor system? At a motel? My god—she hadn't seen *anything* on the honor system since grade school, when her dad would slip a newspaper out of the stack in front of The Sugar Bowl on his way to work before Mr. Lister opened mornings and put his dime on top of the stack. Or no—there was also that roadside vegetable and fruit stand up near Uncle Ed's place by the lake, where everything was priced and you just took whatever produce you wanted and left your money in a cardboard seed box on a rickety wooden table.

But a motel? With a bar? *In the year 2003?*

She couldn't believe it.

She walked over to the key rack.

Evidently she had her choice of rooms. Every niche had a key in it.

It felt strange, knowing she'd be the only guest. Knowing she was all alone. She wondered if she was even safe here. She was out in the middle of nowhere after all. You could disappear from a place like this and nobody'd ever know. She reached into her bag for the cigarettes and lit one and considered her situation.

The alternative was to get back on the road again. The alternative sucked. And if the rooms had keys then they had locks to go with those keys. She thought that would probably do, that if the windows locked she'd probably be all set. And she *did* like this honor system thing. It reminded her of simpler times, quieter times, when neighbors were really neighbors to each another and not just the people next door. When you didn't have to worry about locks and keys.

She'd always been partial to the number three.

Three it is then, she thought. *Time to explore.*

She took the key off the rack and walked outside into the cold night air.

Number three was in the center to her right. A distance of about five feet separated it from the cabin on either side. She liked the old-fashioned look of the cabins right away—dark clapboard siding, shake roofs—most motels these days were nothing more than subdivided bunkers. And then when she stepped inside she was grinning ear to ear.

She had a fireplace!

No television, not even a phone. But a brick-and-mortar fireplace opposite the bed complete with wrought-iron grate, mesh screen, andirons and a small stack of split wood and kindling.

A fireplace, in Florida! Where you might only want one a month or two every year, if that. This was great!

She checked the windows on either side. Locked. She checked the bathroom. It was neat and clean. She had water pressure in the tub and sink and the water warmed up quickly. The toilet flushed. There was soap and shampoo and even a complementary comb, toothbrush and tube of toothpaste on the sink.

What-U-Need indeed.

She sat down on the bed. Soft but not too soft.

She didn't care at all about a television or even a phone for that matter though it would have been nice to call Aunt Marion. She had a fireplace and a paperback novel in her purse and a good soft bed. All she could ask for.

A glass of wine would work, though. She wondered what the bar was like.

She was still a little shaky from the drive here.

A bar alone? At night? *What the hell,* she thought. *In for a penny, in for a pound.*

She'd expected it to be empty. It wasn't.

Behind the reception desk she opened a door to the right of the cash register and heard music right away—Elvis singing DON'T BE CRUEL—and walked a short narrow well-lit corridor past a door marked *management* and another door marked *rest room* to a third door marked *bar* directly ahead of her.

The bar wasn't much to speak of though it did have some nice old-fashioned touches. Green-hooded lamps hung over each of the four tables, making her think of poker-rooms—though she'd never been in one—old tin serving-trays advertising Keubler Beer and Buckingham Cut Plug Smoking Tobacco and Alderney Sweet Cream Butter were tacked above the double row of bottles along with old faded photos of prizefighters, racehorses, ballplayers, none of whom looked familiar. The bar itself sported a wide brass rail and was polished to a high shine.

At first glance the patrons weren't much to speak of either. Two old men sitting at the end of the bar who looked up and smiled at her when she walked in and three younger men in off-the-rack suits and ties talking at one of the tables—who didn't acknowledge her at all—a middle aged heavy-set woman nearest the door who appeared to be drinking whiskey neat from a tumbler and another, younger woman of roughly her own age in the middle of the bar, sipping a glass of red wine. She saw that there was a second glass, as yet untouched, in front of her. Both women nodded and the younger one, a curly-haired redhead, smiled. Lin smiled back and stepped up beside her.

"Evening," she said.

"Hi there," said the woman.

"Anyone sitting here?"

"Nope. It's all yours."

She sat down.

"You got to help yourself, hon," said the other woman. She seemed to be studying her whiskey. "No barkeep."

"Oh, right. Thanks."

She glanced at the two old men down at the end. "Don't mind Pete and Willie," said the redhead. "They're harmless."

Pete and Willie smiled at her again as she rounded the service area and began checking out the bottles.

"Watcha lookin' for, miss?" said the thinner and scruffier of the two. "Maybe I can help."

"White wine?"

"Icebox, right over there." He pointed.

Icebox? She hadn't heard that in years. Where did these people come from, anyway? Her own car was the only one in the driveway. She guessed they'd parked around back somewhere. They did seem friendly enough, though. It had worried her a bit, walking into the bar alone. But she wasn't feeling threatened here.

They didn't have much selection. They had a Rhine wine and a Chablis, a rose and a couple of inexpensive champagnes. She didn't like rose and since the Chablis was open she chose that, found a glass on the shelf behind her and poured. She walked over and set the glass down between the redhead and the older woman.

"Might as well do what I do, pour yourself another while you're back there," said the redhead. "No bartender, right? And hell, it's all on the house."

"I thought that was just soft drinks. Wine's two dollars, right?"

The woman smiled.

"Suppose you're right, though. Save myself a walk. Can I get either of you anything?"

"Could do with another Johnnie," said the older woman.

"Johnnie?"

"Johnnie Walker red. Right behind you. No ice."

She poured the scotch and another glass of wine and set them on the bar and walked back the way she'd come.

Pete and Willie smiled again. The men at the table were still deep in conversation and didn't seem to notice her at all. It was probably just as well. She figured them for salesmen. Except for the sandy-haired one, too much oil in their hair, too many rings on their fingers. Guys with wide lapels and thin ties hitting on her was not on her agenda tonight or ever.

She lit a cigarette and sipped her chardonnay.

"Not bad," she said.

"No," said the redhead. "They got a nice stock in this place."

"You from around here?"

"Lauderdale originally. You staying at the What-U-Need?"

"Uh-huh. I can't believe they have fireplaces. And this whole honor system thing, you know? I mean now? In this day and age? It's amazing."

She smiled again, nodded.

Elvis fell silent a moment and then switched to "Are You Lonesome Tonight."

"I remember when I was a girl," said the older woman, "Philbert's grocery had this big old ice-chest outside filled with chipped ice and soda pop. This was way before them soda-machines. Thing was big as a coffin. Didn't have no room for it in the store so what you'd do is, you'd open it up and take yourself a soda pop and go pay for it inside."

"Heard this one before, Harriet," said the redhead.

"I know you have but she hasn't. One day I didn't have the dime. So I just took one and walked away with it. I figured, nobody around to see. Problem was old man Philbert happened to peek out the window just then looking for his delivery boy. I tell you, my daddy took the strap to me so bad it was a week before I could sit down to table. I shoulda known. See what I'm saying? I shoulda known."

"What room you in?" said the redhead.

"Three."

"Nice room. I'm in six myself."

"Eight," said the older woman. "Harriet Peasely. Pleased to make your acquaintance."

"Linda Wright. Lin."

"I'm Amanda."

They shook hands all around.

"I don't get it," she said, "I thought I was the only person staying here."

"Nah. I think we're pretty well full up in fact, wouldn't you say, Harriet?"

"Pretty near, I guess"

"But the keys..."

"What keys?"

"The keys in the key rack, out there in the office. It's full."

Amanda shrugged. "Duplicates, I guess. Why?"

"But that doesn't make sense. I mean, what if I'd decided on number eight or six, say—your rooms—instead of three? Or any other for that matter?"

She laughed. "I guess somebody would have been pretty surprised, wouldn't they."

It didn't make sense at all. They hadn't been duplicates. There was only one key per niche. She felt *down the rabbit hole* all of a sudden.

"Okay, but then where is everybody? *Where are all the...?*"

And she was about to say cars when the sandy-haired man at the table shouted *fuck it, fuck it! I'm outta here!* his face an angry blotchy red and his chair clattering to the floor behind him and she saw that all three men were on their feet now, the other two trying to restrain the guy, taking hold of his arms. She heard one of them say something like, *you just gotta accept what you did, John, you just gotta* something or other trying to calm and quieten him but the man twisted suddenly in their grasp and shugged them off him and then he was moving fast in her direction, headed for the door. His eyes caught her own.

"So what the fuck are *you* looking at?" he said.

And then he was gone.

The other two men sat down again, shaking their heads. They resumed their conversation.

"What was *that* all about?" she said.

"Nothing you need to worry about, Lin," Amanda said. "He just does that sometimes. He'll get over it. Always does."

"You all *know* one another?"

"Not everybody. I do know John, though."

Maybe it was the glass of wine she'd already finished but this was all getting to be just a bit too much for her. On top of an exhausting day, a damn sight too much. That fire, that nice soft bed—they simply beckoned. She'd work it all out in the morning. Or she wouldn't as the case may be. She needed to get some sleep.

She slid off the barstool and picked up her second glass of wine.

"Think I'll take this with me. I've really got to get some rest, you know? It was nice meeting you."

"Nice meeting you too, Lin," said Amanda. "See you tomorrow night?"

"No. I'm leaving first thing in the morning. Good talking to you, though."

Amanda just smiled again.

"You take care, now," said Harriet. Her second scotch was already half gone. "You take good care now, hear me?"

"Thanks. I will. 'Night."

And it was only when she was outside and halfway to her cabin that she realized she hadn't paid for her drinks. Oh, well, she thought, she'd leave the price of the drinks in the register in the morning along with the rent money. Come to think of it she couldn't remember seeing a second register in the bar so maybe that was what you were supposed to do anyway. Strange way to run a business, though. Strange place all around.

By the time she had the fire going, filling the room with warmth and the delightful smell of pine, she'd pretty much forgotten all about the bar. She didn't even bother opening her paperback. She just lay there between the sheets staring at the flames, worrying about Joel and her uncle and sipping at the wine until in a little while sleep claimed her.

In the morning she showered and dressed and used the complementary toothbrush and toothpaste and towel-dried her hair. She felt refreshed and ready to go. The scent of fire lingered in the room so that she almost hated to leave it. She put two dollars on the end table for the maid and stepped out into the chill of morning.

There was a surprise waiting for her at the reception desk.

A registry book. Bound in black leather—and evidently brand new. It lay open to the first page and there wasn't an entry in it. She signed her name and guessed her check-in time to be about twelve-fifteen a.m. and then looked at her watch. It was ten twenty-five. She wrote down ten twenty-five as her check-out time. Then she went to the register. She depressed the OPEN key and got another surprise.

It was empty.

She'd expected it would at least have held change for a twenty. A twenty was all she had. What the hell, she thought, fifteen for the room, four for the drinks and *a single to the invisible barman.* She put the twenty in the till and closed the drawer. She punched in $20.00 and hit TOTAL and the drawer popped out again so she closed it again and then read the audit strip to be sure it had recorded the amount correctly. She smiled. It was quite an audit strip.

It read *$20.00, payment on the honor system. We have what we need. You've got What-U-Need. Have a nice day.*

She still was smiling when she walked out the door.

"It just happened," said her aunt. "Just like that! One minute he's god knows where and the next he's asking me what time it is, like he's got some lunch date or something...I was so surprised I actually looked at my watch and told him. I said, why, it's ten twenty-five, Ed! And now look at the big dope. Look at him smiling. He scared all of us half to death and now he's smiling like it's Christmas morning!"

"It is Christmas morning," said her uncle. "My favorite niece is here. Gimme a hug, Lin."

She was so relieved she was shaking with laughter and crying at the same time.

"Hey. Does your favorite nephew get in on that too?" She turned and there was Joel behind her, standing smiling in the open doorway.

"He sure as hell does. Come here, you two."

And it was only as she released him and turned to hug her brother too that she thought of exactly what she had been doing at ten twenty-five that morning and then of the audit strip on the register at the What-U-Need Motel.

She drove State Road 70 a number of times after that in both daylight and nighttime and never saw it again. It didn't surprise her. She wondered where it was now and where Amanda and Harriet and the others were now and resolved that if she ever had a child he or she would know all about the honor system in the old days and the new and be careful not to flaunt it.

Thanks to C. for the notion.

My friend Carolyn Kessaratos Shea once worked as a saleswoman driving though New England and she was stunned one night to find herself at a motel out in the sticks somewhere that actually operated on the honor system. Said it was one of the spookiest and most delightful experiences of her life.

Driving Florida's SR70 alone in the fog at night was one of the most unnerving experiences of *my* life. I wanted a place to stop so badly that I could've pulled into the Bates Motel without a qualm. But unless you counted the trucks roaring by there wasn't a single sign of human habitation for miles.

There was roadkill everywhere I looked including the deer carcass directly in front of me in the headlights—and that goddamn rabbit damn near killed me.

I put the two together and sprinkled in a barfull of ghosts.

—JK

Lighten Up

It was about 11:30 and Adoni was messing with the lighting again. The lighting was track lighting and he was forever adjusting it slightly downward. Up a little here, down a little there but mostly down. By ten or so it was nearly impossible to read the menu. The consensus among us was that that was the idea. He wasn't making the place any more romantic. He was making it cavernous. You couldn't read, you couldn't order. Time to go home.

Joe, Michael, Robert, Amy and I were all a little drunk so we didn't mind the gloom. Gert was already so far gone she could barely talk and when she did talk you had no reason to listen to her. Behind the bar Stella kept pouring. The music was so familiar we could probably have sung along without knowing a single word of Greek.

Night at the *Santorini.*

The conversation had descended into rarely known facts. Or maybe barely known facts was more appropriate because you could bet that some of this was bullshit. Sure, an ostrich's eye is bigger than its brain and butterflies taste with their feet. But is it *really* impossible to sneeze with your eyes open?

I needed proof on that one. Unfortunately none of us had allergies.

"Okay, did you know that 'stewardesses' is the longest word you can type using only your *left* hand and 'lollipop' the longest using your right?"

Michael was a writer so we had to believe him there.

"And that the average person's left hand does most of the typing?"

"Nah, why would that be?" said Joe.

Joe worked with computers all day, setting up online systems for hotels and motels, so he'd logged in plenty of time at the keyboard himself.

"Dunno. Just is."

"Even if you're right-handed?"

"Yep."

"Doesn't make sense."

"Palindromes," said Robert. He sipped his beer. It was probably his seventh.

"What?"

"*Palindromes*. Racecar. Kayak. Level."

"What the hell's he talking about?" said Amy.

Robert tended to be strange and mysterious now and then so you never knew.

"They're the same whether you write them right to left, or left to right," said Michael. "That's what he means."

"*Thassright,*" said Robert. "Palindromes."

"What's that got to do with your left hand doing most of the typing?" said Joe.

"Absolutely nothing."

" 'The quick brown fox jumps over the lazy dog,' uses every letter in the alphabet," said Amy. "We learned that back in typing class. And you know what else? There's no Betty Rubble in Flintstones Chewable Vitamins."

"Jesus wept," said Joe.

He looked at me. "I need a smoke," he said. "You ready?"

"I'm gonna wait a while. Finish my scotch. It's fuckin' *cold* out there."

"I know it's fuckin' cold out there." He was already putting on his coat.

"Fuckin' *cold* out there," said Gert.

We ignored her.

"Amy?" said Joe.

"I'll wait."

"Michael?"

"Same here."

"Fuckin' Bloomberg," said Joe.

"You got that right," I said.

"Fuckin' Bloomberg!" said Gert.

It was practically a mantra by now. *Fuckin' Bloomberg.* Since the smoking ban in New York City bars, we citizens who favored our tar and nicotine had to step outside evenings for a smoke and now the weather had turned cold on us. Bloomberg was going to freeze our little subculture to death if he had his way.

Even those of us regulars who didn't smoke hated the sonovabitch if only for interrupting our conversation.

I watched him drift out the door. Behind him a couple from the tables was leaving too. The tables were empty now in fact except for one other couple by the far right window. The only patrons of *Santorini* were the two of them, us down at the far end of the bar, two young Spanish guys at the front end hitting on a lovely young brunette who seemed to like their attention and a pair of yuppie types—a man and a woman, probably in their mid-thirties—talking earnestly about something or other in between. I saw Joe's match flare and die behind the plate-glass.

"Babies are born without kneecaps," said Robert. "Really?"

"Really. You don't develop them until you're about two or something."

"So if you want to get in trouble with the mob," I said, "the thing to do is to do it *early.*"

"Exactly."

"No word in the English language rhymes with 'month'," said Michael.

"*Dunth,*" lisped Robert.

"Or 'orange'."

"*Porridge,*" said Robert.

"Doesn't count," I said. "No *ng* sound."

"Or 'silver'."

"Hi-yo to that!"

"Or 'purple'."

"*Splurpable.* Like Amy."

"You really are a *dunth,*" said Amy.

We listened to the music for a while.

The door opened and it wasn't Joe but some other guy, heavy-set, in a woolen coat much too thin for the weather. He sat down between us and the yuppies. He looked half-frozen and rubbed his bare hands together vigorously, smiled and ordered a Heineken.

Stella set the bottle down in front of him along with a frozen mug the guy obviously didn't much need. He poured anyway, took a sip and set it down. Then he fished in his pocket and came out with a pack of Winstons and a clear plastic lighter. He lit up.

"Check this out," I said.

And then it was *eyes left* for all of us.

It took the yuppies a couple of puffs to get a whiff of it. Concerned glances were exchanged. Looks of disgust. It was the woman—not the guy she was with—who finally stepped up to the plate.

"Excuse me? Sir? You can't smoke in here," she said. "It's against the law."

"Uh-huh."

"Sir?"

The Spanish guys had noticed too. "She's right, man" said the taller of the two, "I could care less, you know? But you get busted, man. You get *fined*. All that bullshit."

"Please put that out," she said. "It's against the law."

"You already said that." He took another drag. *Slowly.*

Adoni stepped in from the kitchen. Like most Greeks he was a smoker too but he had no choice. He was manager. He did his job.

"I'm sorry, but you will have to put that out, my friend," he said. "It's the law."

"Okay," said the guy.

He dropped the butt and stepped on it.

Good choice, I thought. Adoni didn't have a mean bone in his body but he'd been Greek Army in Afghanistan. He was big. He had a grip that could bruise mahogany and though he didn't use it often you wouldn't want to cross him.

"You are from out of town?" he said.

"Nope. Lower East Side. Just wanted to see what you folks'd do." He drank his beer and smiled. "I'm with C.L.A.S.H. We're doing this all over town."

"Clash?"

"Citizens Lobbying Against Smoking Harassment."

"Ah yes, I see. You lobby for smoking. I wish you a very good night, sir. But on this?—you must wait. Enjoy yourself."

"Thank you."

"C.L.A.S.H., huh?" I said. "I've heard of it."

"Lawsuits," said Robert. "That's the ticket."

"We're filing them. Plus a little guerrilla theatre now and then, if you know what I mean."

He winked at us and smiled.

"We wish you all the luck in the world, sir."

Robert raised his glass to the guy. We all did—with the exception of Gert, who was wearing a puzzled expression. As though we'd all turned to Steuben glass figures suddenly and she couldn't for the life of her understand how or why.

Joe came back in and the yuppie made a face as he passed her. I guess she noticed he'd been smoking. "...*bet his mouth smells like an ashtray...*" I heard her mutter. I guess I was the only one who did. It got a smile out of her partner.

But she was beginning to piss me off.

"I'm Jerzy," I said and offered my hand to the C.L.A.S.H. guy. "This is Joe, Robert, Amy and Michael." I didn't bother with Gert. Gert was puzzled.

"I'm Art," he said. We shook hands all around.

I saw that the table was paying Rita. She moved off to get them change. The Spanish guys had already settled up with Stella and they were smiling, herding the pretty young brunette out the door. I judged her slightly sloshed. One of them just might get lucky tonight if they didn't both blow it with too much eager competition.

I ordered another scotch. So did Joe and Michael. Amy finished her red wine and ordered another. Robert was still sipping his beer. He licked the foam off his mustache. The C.L.A.S.H. guy, Art, asked for another Heineken. The couple beside us ordered too—theirs was the house white. Of course it was.

Stella poured, quickly and efficiently. You had to love the woman.

"I got one for you," said Joe. "Thought of it outside. Did you know that Al Capone's business card said he was a used furniture dealer?"

"I did not," said Robert.

"Did you know that our eyes stay exactly the same size from birth," said Amy, "but our noses and ears never stop growing?"

"I did not," said Robert.

Maybe that was why Gert was looking at us so strangely. Maybe she was watching our ears grow.

"Did you know that Adoni has just locked the front door?" said Michael.

It was true. The couple from the table had just stepped out the door and Adoni'd locked it behind them. He was walking toward us, smiling, digging in his shirt pocket.

"If you got them, light them," he said.

He put a cigarette in his mouth, walked by us and disappeared in back.

I lit up. Michael and Amy lit up. Art lit up. Joe lit up even though he'd only just had one. Robert didn't smoke. Gert fumbled around in her pocketbook for a while and then even she managed it.

The couple beside us looked aghast—like they'd maybe seen a ghost. *The ghost of barrooms past.*

"I don't believe this," said the guy.

"You realize this is against the law?" said the woman. There it was—the law again. The woman was obsessed.

"A man's bar is his castle," said Robert.

"This is a public space," the man said. "There are staff here. Waitresses, cooks, busboys. Not to mention how rude this is to us."

"He's gonna mention second-hand smoke any minute," said Joe to me sotto voce.

"Second-hand smoke has been proven to..."

"I told ya," said Joe.

"Second-hand smoke!" said Gert. "That's right." There was lipstick on her Virginia Slim.

"We have every right to demand you put them out right away," said the woman.

"That's right," said Art. "You do."

"Then in that case we would you please put them out right away."

"Sorry, but no," Michael said.

Adoni walked in. You could hear his pockets jingling. There was a Marlboro fired up in the corner of his mouth. "There is a problem?" he said.

"We've asked these people to put their cigarettes out and I'll ask you to do the same. This is outrageous! Does your owner know about this?"

"The owner is Greek," he shrugged. "A smoker, sorry to say."

"We have just ordered drinks. We have every right to be able to drink our drinks in peace without having to deal with smoke being blown in our faces."

"Face away from the smoke, then. That is the solution."

"Don't you get it?" said the man. "We could have you *closed down* for this!"

"I don't think so. For first offense, they fine you."

"*Fined*, then."

"I don't think so."

He took the handcuffs out of his pocket, snapped one on the guy's right wrist and the other to the shiny brass bar-rail. The guy barely knew what hit him. His lady friend slid off the barstool purse in hand with the clear intent of heading for the door away from all these lunatics but Amy was there in front of her and so was I and Adoni made short work of cuffing her to the rail too. He seated them both back down.

We knew the drill pretty well by then so Amy went through the woman's purse for her wallet while I dug his out of his inside jacket pocket. I handed it to Michael, more for show of solidarity than anything else. He read off the driver's license.

"James Wade Holt," he said. "Hey, you're a neighbor! 175 West 69th Street."

Amy was reading the woman's. She shook her head. "They don't live together," she said. "This one's 33 West 48th Street—Hell's Kitchen. Joanna Bowen."

"Why do we have a tendency not to give women middle names in this country?" said Robert. "I've always wondered about that. This one's James Wade Holt and this one's just plain Joanna. Doesn't seem fair."

"No, it doesn't," Joe said.

"*What...what are you doing? What are you going to do to us?*" said James Wade Holt.

The woman said nothing, only looked around anxiously from face to face.

"Did you know a dragonfly has a life span of only twenty-four hours?" said Michael.

"I did not," said Robert.

"Stella? Give me a check pad, please," said Adoni.

She handed him the pad. We handed him the wallets. He took a pen out of his shirt pocket and opened them and started writing. The place was totally silent. Somebody—probably Stella—had turned off the bouzouki music. When he was finished he closed the wallets up again and put them on the bar.

"First of all," he said. "You will not report this. You see, I have your names and addresses. I will make copies for all my friends here so that they will have them too. You do not have *their* names or addresses, however. So if anything should happen to me or to the restaurant *Santorini* they will know where to find you. In a moment I will release you and you will finish your glasses of wine and you will each have another, on me, on the house. We will smoke because that is what smokers do and you will not complain. You will be our guests."

"A crocodile," said Robert, "cannot stick out its tongue."

"What if we simply want to leave?" said just plain Joanna. "I mean, what if James and I..."

"You will not leave until we say so. We have done this many times, you see. Do not think you are the first to act as you have acted and be inconvenienced for it. If you had simply said nothing and walked away thinking *live and let live*, then fine. But you did not. You will not be harmed but you will endure what we have had to endure and feel like a second-class citizen in your own city. It may make you angry. It makes us angry. But that is life, no? And when you leave here you can forget all about this. A goldfish, after all, has a memory span of approximately three seconds."

He unlocked the cuffs.

"Enjoy yourselves," he said. "I will go and Xerox the copies."

"You guys are amazing," said Art. He laughed. "I'm putting this little tactic up on the website."

"No names, no places," I said.

"Goes without saying."

"Not a single study, by the way, has validated the claim that second-hand smoke can be dangerous to humans," said Robert. "What is certain is that your clothes are going to stink a little. Mine always do. But hell, what are friends for?"

The couple said nothing. They sipped their drinks. I saw that the woman's hands were still shaking. I didn't mind.

"Did you know that cats have over a hundred vocal sounds, and dogs only around ten?" he said.

"Ten!" said Gert. "Ten dogs!"

Our personal captivity wore on.

When thanks to Mayor Bloomberg not smoking became *verboten* in New York bars a lot of us, shall we say, resented it a little. Just a little. Hardly worth mentioning. Honest.

And a lot of us who hated holier-than-thou yuppie-types dreamed dreams just like this one.

—JK

Hotline

He put the phone down in its cradle on the desk and sat back in the wooden armchair—its springs creaked. The springs annoyed him. If he held onto this job for any time at all he'd have to remember to bring in the 3-in-1 oil.

In his crossword puzzle he was stuck on a nine-letter word for *shapeless*. All he had was a final S.

Four calls, he thought, in a little over two hours, the first two hours of his very first solo shift. *Damn! people were depressed these days.* He'd taken the training and asked a few questions but obviously he hadn't asked one of the important ones—just what was the volume anyway?

He hadn't expected it to be this heavy.

If grief were cash he'd be looking at a windfall here.

Could be it was the storm outside. A heavy cold March rainfall. He could hear it pounding at the windows of the Y. The storm wanted in.

A low barometer was called a *depression*, wasn't it?

He wondered if there was a connection.

Connection. Another interesting word, given what he was doing.

He was considering an expressly forbidden trip to the men's room for a Winston when the phone rang again.

"Crisis Center Hotline," he said. "How can I help you?"

"I've been...I'm thinking that..."

The voice was agitated, thin. Male.

"Yes?"

"I'm thinking that maybe I ought to kill myself."

"Why would you want to do that, sir? Talk to me about it. That's what I'm here for."

He sighed. "Okay. All right. It's been nine whole months since Barbara left and I still can't put it behind me—that last conversation, those last couple of days, I still can't stop thinking about her. Jesus, nine whole months! You'd think I'd be over it by now, wouldn't you? What do you call it? Reconciled? I mean, people have *babies* in nine months! I get up in the morning and the first thing I do is check my e-mail, thinking maybe there'll be a message from her. Something. There never is. I'm constantly depressed. My sleep-pattern's a goddamn wreck. I don't eat enough, I drink too much. I can't seem to decide what to *do* with myself, y'know?"

"You can't get control of things."

"That's right. That's it exactly. Everything's out of control. You should see me. You really should. I'm a mess! I've gained weight, my immune system's all shot to hell—I've had three colds already this year, herpes sores, the whole bit. Half the time I don't even bother shaving. I can't get into my work god knows..."

"What do you do for a living, sir? If you don't mind my asking."

"I'm a painter."

"A housepainter?"

"No, I paint. I do magazine and book covers. And my own fine art. I've got a gallery here and there. But I can't seem to give a damn about any of it anymore."

"You've lost contact with a lot of your friends, am I right?"

"That's right."

"Are you taking risks? I mean unnecessary risks?"

"Hell, yes. I had to drive into Portland last weekend to pick up some materials, some supplies, you know? *Twice* I walked into oncoming traffic! Then driving back here I had the Buick up to seventy and... well, do you know the area up north of there?"

"Yes, sir, I do, sir. Lived in this area all my life."

"Well, then you know all these blind hills, all these hairpin turns along route 80. A dog, a cat, another car—any one of them could have sent me off the road. I'm not even that good a driver. Look, please don't call me 'sir', okay?"

"All right."

"No offense."

"None taken."

"It reminds me of my father."

"Your father?"

"He always wanted us to call him 'sir.' Know what I mean? So I'm supposed to be a painter, right?"

"Uh-huh."

"Well, what I'm just trying to say here, it seems as though since Barbara left, everything's completely *drained* of color. Everything's gray. No color at all. It's like the best of me, of my life, she took away with her. Like she took something I honestly can't get back again. That I'll never get back again. Like there's no point. Like the best of me's past and gone now. You see what I'm saying?"

"You can't stop the pain. And you can't see a future without it."

"That's right."

He leaned forward, elbows on the desk. The chair creaked again. The rain pounded. They'd told him during the training sessions that just the act of talking to someone could temporarily change perspective, offer a reprieve, that simple human contact actually had the power to alter brain chemistry. He didn't know if he believed that but it was time to get cracking.

"Can I ask you, have you given any thought to how you might do this?"

"Do what? Take my life?"

"Yes. You don't have any guns in the house, do you?"

"No."

"That's good. How then?"

"I...I don't know."

"I bet you can't guess what I used to do for a living."

"Excuse me?"

"I'm retired. You know what I used to do for a living?"

"What."

"I was a cop."

"A cop?"

"That's right. Twenty-four years on the highway patrol."

"Really?"

"That's right."

"I don't get it. Why are you telling me this?"

"Because over twenty-four years you see things. A lot of things you don't necessarily want to see. You know in some states attempted suicide's still against the law? It is. And there's a reason for that. Do you know what you goddamn people put us through? You jump off a bridge, we find you gray and blue and bloated in the water. We pick you up, good chance you're gonna explode in our faces or fall the hell apart in our hands. Blow your head off and we pick pieces of you out of the carpet or the grass or scrape what passes for your brains off the goddamn walls. Take a dive off a building you maybe kill a pedestrian, whoops, sorry! we got to figure out who the fuck's who. We pack you in bags, wipe away your vomit and shit and your piss. You miserable sonovabitch. You make somebody else pick up your cold dead guts and you think you're worth the trouble. You want to die? You piece of shit *I* ought to kill you! I'd at least be cleaning up my own mess! *My* mess! Oh, you're such a nice guy, you're hurting, my fucking heart *goes out* to you!"

He could almost hear the pulse racing on the other end of the line and then it went dead. Same as the last four—though the teenage kid had hung up on him halfway through when he told him to stop sucking at his mother's tit. The little prick.

He replaced the receiver.

He knew this couldn't last. How could it? Somewhere along the line somebody, one of these goddamn whiners, was going to decide complaining about him was worth living for and that would be the end of it.

Meantime he figured he was doing a lot of good here.

He suspected he was probably batting four out of five.

He doubted the kid would off himself but then he doubted he'd be the one to do any complaining either.

It was time for that smoke. Hell, he was a volunteer. Screw the rules. He got out of the chair and left the office and walked down the empty hall to the men's room sat in a stall that still reeked of the janitor's morning Lysol and lit up. He listened to the rain and wind outside. He got into a coughing fit which served to remind him he had only one lung left which was why he'd left the HP in the first place. He wondered what he'd do with himself once they kicked him off this job.

Find another crisis center? They sure weren't in short supply.

He flushed the butt and when he got back to the office the phone was ringing.

"Crisis center hotline. How can I help you?"

"I'm about to eat my weapon."

"Excuse me? Say that again?"

"I said I'm about to eat my weapon. What are you, deaf? I just wanted somebody to know. Not that that makes any goddamn difference either."

"Ralph?"

"Huh?"

"Ralph? Is that you?"

"What? Who the fuck is this?"

"Jesus Christ, Ralphy. It's Joe. What the fuck are you *talking* about?"

He'd know his ex-partner's voice over a screaming crowd at Fenway Park.

"Aw, shit, Joe. It fucking figures, you know? I call to tell some anonymous fuck he can shove life up his asshole and I get you of all people. I always said if it wasn't for bad luck I wouldn't have none at all. Proves me out. What the fuck are you doing manning a crisis center? You fucking *hate* people!"

"Jesus, Ralphy. I don't hate *you*! What the hell are you thinking of?"

"I'm takin' the .45 caliber highway, Joe."

"You can't do that!"

"Sure I can. McNulty did, remember? Only his was a .38."

"Wait. I'm coming right over."

"Nah. That's bullshit."

"Don't do anything until I get there. Promise me."

"What? You want to watch? That's my Joey. That's my boy."

"Come on, dammit! Listen to me. Don't *do* anything to yourself! I want you to promise me."

" 'Bye, Joe."

"Wait! For chrissake *wait*!"

"Amazing. Good old Joe Fitzpatrick, model compassionate citizen. Now I seen everything. Now I can fucking die happy."

"Wait, goddammit! Ralph. Ralph!"

But the line was dead and by the time he made it through the goddamn storm so was Ralphy, all over the kitchen floor so he had to call for cleanup.

He knew the number.

I'd read a fascinating oral history by Connie Fletcher called *What Cops Know* and wondered, given their own testimony, how the huge majority of them didn't go completely bonkers. So I posited one who did. And who then got a job on a crisis hotline.

I love irony and black humor and this was a lot of fun to do.

—JK

Monster

I didn't know which one was bigger, the guy walking toward me or his dog.

As they got closer I thought the dog maybe had an edge on him. But you couldn't be sure.

The guy was looking right at me though. Smiling. The dog was looking at me too—all two-hundred or so pounds of him I was guessing. Columbus Avenue is a very busy street at lunchtime weekdays and people were moving by all around me outside the Café. Guys on cell phones. Wives on cell phones. Nannies pushing double-wide strollers. A gorgeous long-legged twenty-something with about a foot of creamy flesh between her halter top and hip-huggers just begging the eye to follow.

Yet these two were focused on me.

I'm pretty uninteresting. Average looks. Average height. Smoking your average filter cigarette.

I didn't know them, that was for sure. I'd have recognized that enormous St. Bernard anywhere. And I'd have known the guy too. His head was as bald as the twenty-something's navel and he was dressed with a kind of offhand rumpled elegance. Think Tom Wolfe—having slept in his clothes all night. But with wrists the size of biceps, thighs thicker than the average guy's waistline and a belly hard as a boulder.

I did know one thing about him. This guy was going to *talk to me*.

I don't know how I knew but I did.

It was questionable for a moment whether I should smile at them in return or run like hell back into the Café and wait for my dessert. In the first place I was in no mood to talk to anybody. Certainly not to a stranger. You never knew what you were going to encounter on the streets of Manhattan or which kind of crazy was going to be grinning at you. What I did was drop my Winston and step on it and by the time I finished that the dog had already loped over and his wet black nose was sniffing at my jeans.

I like dogs. Always have. And this one seemed to like me. Those deep-set big brown eyes told me so.

Oh, what the hell, I thought.

"You mind?"

"'Course not," he said.

I bent down to scratch the massive black-and-white skull and then behind the ears. I didn't have far to bend. I figured him at two-and-a-half feet at the shoulder. Adequate scratching required both hands.

"Aristophanes," said the guy.

"Pleased to meet you, Aristophanes," I said.

The dog shook a little drool off his muzzle and bent his head. My cue to move on down to his neck. Beneath the thick fur I could feel the slabs of muscle hard as a steer's.

"You're a dog person," said the guy. His voice was very soft and you'd have expected a lower pitch from a man his size—easily a six-footer. But there was an easy drawl to it that said the South was in there somewhere. And there was also something else I couldn't quite identify at first. It only came to me later.

"Sure I am."

The dog looked up at me again, nose twitching. I squatted down so that we were pretty much eye to eye. His breath was clean and doggy. I scratched at the dewlap beneath his neck.

"Aristophanes likes you, don't you fella?"

And then my hands were getting washed with extreme prejudice by a dog named after an ancient Greek comedic playwright. When he finally put the tongue away I went back to attending to the dewlap and behind the floppy ears.

"You have a dog yourself?"

I smiled. "No. I used to. My mom's got a dog. I see him from time to time. That's about it. I grew up with dogs when I was a kid, though. The neighborhood was full of them."

"So why not now? You should indulge yourself, my friend."

Under some circumstance I might have found that sort of impertinent I guess you'd say. He didn't know me after all. And it *was* Manhattan. There were rules of the road, rules of conversation. Instead I answered him.

"My work—it wouldn't be fair to a dog. I'm a travel writer. Six months out of a year I'm off somewhere."

"That's too bad," he said.

For a moment I thought he meant the job. That the job was *too bad*. New Yorkers get prickly about such things. But he was talking about having dogs naturally.

"A good dog requires attention," he said.

"Yes. That's true. And space to run around in, too. Something else I don't have. This guy would go crazy in my apartment. You live here in the City?"

I was now actually talking to him. *Engaging* him. It occurred to me to wonder why.

"Most of the time I do. We're lucky, though, Aristophanes and me. I moved here in '72, found myself a good-sized loft down in Soho. We've also got a place out in Connecticut. Sixteen acres there."

Sixteen acres in Connecticut. A Soho loft.

I was speaking to a gentleman of means. I looked at him again and realized that yes, he and Tom Wolfe could have easily had the same tailor.

I scratched the broad sloping shoulders. Scratched hard to get through the thick brown and white fur. He was a beauty. Groomed to the nines. He let out what sounded like a groan of pleasure.

The man laughed.

And then suddenly I knew one more thing. Just as a moment ago I'd known he was going to talk to me.

This guy was going to touch me too.

Nobody touches a stranger in New York.

Nobody. Never.

He reached down and placed his hand on my shoulder. "You'll have a dog one day," he said. "You'll see."

There is only one word I can think of to this day to express the touch of that hard wide hand. It was what I'd sensed before when he called me a dog person.

Benevolence.

And the hand felt for all the world like a kind of benediction.

I was shocked. I think I tried to stammer something.

But the dog put a stop to that. Energetically.

He licked my face with his warm wet tongue from chin to forehead until I was laughing so hard I was in danger of falling over out of my squat so I stood up and wiped my face. The man was laughing too. He gave the leash a light tug.

"You have a good day now, " he said. "Good to meet you."

"Good to meet you too," I said. "You too, Aristophanes. He really is a comedian, isn't he?" I wiped my face again.

"A *playwright*," he said, "of the very best kind," and slowly walked away.

I went back into the crowded noisy Café meaning to head straight for the men's room to wash up dog-spit but on impulse turned instead. There was this strange sense of *knowing* again purring in my brain. So I peered out through the doorway in the direction they'd headed and there they were facing me, the big man waving just as I'd known he would and the big dog looking at me and cocking his head as if to say *well, what did you expect?*

Instead of coffee I ordered a single-malt whiskey with my crème brûlée. It was an impulse. A tiny celebration.

I never saw the two of them again.

At home that evening when Dorothy seemed to want to go on with our fight from the night before I barely listened.

I met the antithesis of Aristophanes about a year later. In Greece of all places. On the island of Mykonos.

Once again I was really in no mood for strangers.

A lot about the travel-guide and travel-writing business had changed since I started working for the *Let's Go!* and *Dollar-a-Day* Guides and the occasional *Fodor's* freelance job back in the seventies. Computers had made everything easier. Whole sections of the guides—the *getting there* sections for instance, keeping up with site hours, admission fees, currency conversions, that kind of thing— could be updated yearly by simply consulting the net and recording the facts accordingly.

What you still needed legwork for was to look in on the continued quality—or utter vanishing—of hotels, restaurants, services. Or in places that had become a bit dodgy for tourists of late via natural or man-made disasters you wanted somebody to count the guns so to speak. And of course if you were doing an article for the *New York Times* or the *Washington Post* or one of the better magazines you normally had to be there.

I didn't much like computers so at the age of forty-nine I was still racking up the frequent-flyer miles as much as kids half my age.

It was the source of most of the problems between my longtime lady Dorothy and me. I was still on the road half the time. My *New York Times* press pass didn't impress her one bit.

Dorothy hated flying.

And she was not going to move in with somebody who walked in, dropped his bags, wrote for a week or two and then took off again. When we fought it always ended the same way. I was a selfish bastard who refused to grow up. She was a smothering bitch. I could get mean.

At the time my bread-and-butter client was the *Passport Guides* series, with offices out of London, Paris, Melbourne and New York. Our yearly updates were assigned to six field writers per guide, one more at the computer and a pair of stay-at-home editors. This year our country was Greece—in which we each had some expertise—and while my colleagues were busy on the mainland, the Peloponnese and other of the island chains my own territory was the Cyclades and the Ionian Sea.

I'd already finished the Ionian and Mykonos was my third stop in the Cyclades after Andros and Tinos. All routine thus far.

It was mid-March, headed for Greek Easter and there was still a chill in the air.

The food at the Avra had been fine though overpriced and the room too brightly lit to my taste and you couldn't help but despair a little at the presence of schnitzel on the menu and beefburger Roquefort. I stopped in for a couple of definitely overpriced drinks at Pierro's and then headed up through town to Little Venice and circled around to the windmills.

It was still the best part of Mykonos if you were an old hand like me. The windmills hadn't changed even if much of the rest of the island seemed to want to be Paris-on-the-Aegean. They sat overlooking the dark gleam of sea as bravely as they had for decades. I sat down on the rocks near the one farthest from the square and the music and considered the life I'd made for myself thus far.

Scotch can do that to me.

I had work which I usually enjoyed—though god knows not always—and which provided me with more freedoms than most people had and a more than adequate income. I had an intelligent handsome woman who loved me but whose creature-comforts I had for many years been unresponsive to in all honesty. I had health and reasonable vigor. I had a well-loved mother in her late seventies going steadily blind with retinitis pigmentosa in suburban New Jersey who saw the world as though through a soda straw but who asked little of me other than the occasional visit with her and her dog Beau and a postcard to add to her collection.

I had people who welcomed me warmly scattered all around the globe but few who could do so genuinely, who didn't also view me with some suspicion and in some cases downright fear.

I considered all this. And I wondered about my *usefulness* in general.

A few years down the road as computers more and more peeked into every corner on earth—and in real time at that—it might be possible to eliminate folks like me entirely. Or at least cut our number to the absolute bone. I felt that I'd gone almost *abstract* somehow—as though, like the windmills, my original function had possibly long since ceased and was now more in the nature of the decorative and even metaphoric. I was the friend, the acquaintance, the boyfriend, the son, the travel writer.

I was a brand-name, a label.

I got up and went looking for a quiet bar where they still had real *bouzouki* on the tape or CD player and by the time I found one up in the hills it was late and by the time I had two or three Metaxas it was later still. I was pleasantly lost as you tend to get in Mykonos' winding maze of streets even after many visits and pleasantly buzzed from the Metaxa. I meandered along, taking my good time about it. If I kept heading basically downhill toward the port I'd find my room eventually.

Crime wasn't a problem on Mykonos so neither was the fact that I was alone.

At least not until I saw the dog.

I turned a corner and he froze me in my tracks.

He was peering at me from where he lay on a low stone step maybe twenty-five feet away. If I'd had the feeling of instant good will from Aristophanes back in New York I had exactly the opposite feeling from this one.

This dog hated me on sight.

Or maybe it was the sound of my steps or the smell of me he hated.

Because he couldn't have had much vision left. The cataracts on both his eyes focused a dull opalesque gleam on me in the light from the porch above. I thought inanely for a moment of the statues of blind Homer. Eyes molded flat and empty. Eyes that could stare forever.

In The Iliad *dogs scavenged the bodies of fallen Troy.*

And just as I knew Aristophanes' owner was going to talk to me and touch me that day I knew that this dog and I were going to have our own kind of conversation.

He stood slowly and never took his eyes off me and if an animal can rise in total threat that was what he did. He seemed to unfold from the stone itself like some ugly black gargoyle brought to life with teeth already bared.

He wasn't huge but he wasn't some cocker spaniel either. Maybe three feet long from nose to tail. So skinny you could count his ribs. His coat was thin, short. Patchy-looking, dull and dirty. The fur along his backbone bristled.

When he started to move I put my hands slowly into the pockets of my jeans and waited. He didn't so much walk to me as glide in my direction. As though the air between us were thick as mud. His claws on the fieldstone footpath didn't make a sound. There was just that low quiet growl.

I guess I expected him to stop at some point, prepare to take a leap at me or maybe take a run at me, and in either case that was when the hands came out of the pockets and I'd step back for what I could only pray would be a good solid kick.

But he did neither.

He just kept coming. Until I could have reached down and patted his scarred matted head. Which would have been a very good way to lose a hand at the wrist. And he stared. Not so much as a blink. The growl got louder and so did the pulse throbbing in my ears.

Then he opened his mouth.

And very carefully and purposefully bit.

He bit my thigh just above the knee. Not hard enough to reach the flesh beneath but hard enough to pinch and increase the pressure of the pinch so as to succeed in intimidating the hell out of me. Hard enough to let me know he was *there* goddammit and not some figment of my imagination. He bit *malevolently*, his pale eyes never even twitching, growling all the time—and the thought went through my mind that this was good for him, he was somehow *enjoying* this, to him this was wonderful. That he was getting even for god knows what offenses against his person or how many times or when or where, taking it all out on a total stranger in the silence of a dimly lit pathway late into the lonely night.

I let him bite. I had no choice. I never made a move. In his awful way he was as huge to me as Aristophanes.

A moment later he released me. Turned and walked away as though I were of no consequence whatever nor had ever been. As though I weren't there.

I couldn't trust a dog after that.

I avoided them on the street unless they were so small as to barely qualify as dogs at all. The others I gave a wide berth.

I knew it was irrational. I just couldn't help it.

That black seemed to sidle up to me every time.

The only one I did trust was my mother's dog. An unshaven miniature poodle I'd known for years. Beau and I were old buddies. I fed him scraps of steak and fries from the dinner-table. When I slept over I'd awake with him sleeping at my feet. No way in the world he was ever going to bite anybody and certainly not me.

He could barely see to bite anyway.

It was the only thing he had in common with that creature in Mykonos.

His blindness wasn't due to cataracts though. It had the same inherited root as my mother's—retinitis pigmentosa—what begins as a kind of night-blindness slowly narrows your field of vision on each side and up and down until all you can see is what's directly in front of you. Tunnel vision. Quarter-size down to nickel-size down to dime-size and finally down to nothing at all.

My mother's hadn't progressed that far.

Beau's had. He was sensitive to changes in light but that was all.

It was uncanny—my mother and I both thought so, like that old saw about owners and their dogs starting to look alike—but he also had dangerously high blood pressure and so did she. Like her, he was on medication for it. Which worked most of the time. But since his meds went into his food it all depended on his appetite. Sometimes between the retinitis and the meds not quite taking and a poodle's somewhat hyper temperament in the first place he'd be bouncing off walls.

Literally.

Over the past few years he'd chipped or knocked out several teeth.

But she and the dog were alone and they were crazy about one another. My mother's feeling was—meds, vets, dental work—whatever it took. She worried about the pain of course. Broken teeth. Bloody nose. I did too. He was a sweet-minded animal who still leapt yipping at me when I walked through the door like the pup he was when she first brought him home.

But the vast majority of the time he still seemed like a happy animal, however grotesque these occasional accidents had become.

I'd been in Nice for a while, doing a piece for the *Times* on the restorations there, when I got a call from her. I had only returned the day before and I was jet-lagged as hell and exhausted. The trip had come hard on the heels of a *Post* article on the remote Yaeyama Islands in the Okinawa chain. One day it seemed I'd be looking at water buffalo and mangrove swamps and the next, string bikinis along the private beach at the Hotel Beau Rivage.

I wondered how much longer I could go on like this.

"I want you to come see Beau," she said. Her voice sounded shaky.

"What's going on?"

"Can you come tomorrow? He's...he's just not right. I want you to see him for yourself."

She was scaring me a little.

"Hell mom, I'll drive in tonight if you want."

"No! Tomorrow! Come in tomorrow. There's something..."

"What?"

"There's something I want you to do for me."

"All right. Sure. I'll be there by noon, okay? Are you all right, mom? You don't sound good."

"I will be. I will be now I think. Thank you, Rob. See you tomorrow."

"What was that about?" said Dorothy. She was cleaning up takeout from Chirping Chicken.

"I dunno. Something's going on with the dog. She wouldn't say. She sounded upset though."

"You want me to come along?"

"Don't you have a bunch of fourth-graders to deal with?"

She shrugged. "I can take a mental-health day. If you want."

I thought about it. "No, that's all right. I'll handle it myself."

I was shutting her out again. I knew that. But I didn't want her there. I didn't know why but I didn't.

I arranged for a ten-thirty pickup at Avis the next day and by quarter after eleven pulled into our driveway. I'd grown up in this house and lived here all through college and knew every inch of it like I knew my own apartment. Yet there was a stillness about it today as I climbed the steps that seemed somehow unfamiliar. I almost wouldn't have been surprised see it stripped of furniture. But I opened the front door and there was my mother rising to a sitting position on the worn old couch she still refused to part with, fumbling for her glasses and I realized simultaneously that she'd been asleep this late in the day which was not at all her habit and that Beau hadn't come to greet me which definitely was his.

"Mom? What's happening? What's going on?"

She focused on me and her face seemed to break apart from the center outward like a broken mirror.

Her arm swept low across the room.

"Look!" she said. "Just look."

The walls and baseboards in the living room were white. She'd had them painted white over my objections—I'd argued for natural wood. Now, by the fireplace, on each side of the television set, at the foot of the couch, in the corner behind the end-table, they were smeared and flecked with brown.

"Is that...?

"*Yes. It's blood!*" she wailed. "It's his blood. I don't understand it. My god! He's trying to *kill himself!*"

My mother was not a hysterical woman. She sounded like one now.

I went to her and wrapped my arms around her and let her cry it out awhile. She smelled like sleep and old tears. I felt miserable for her. *Poor little boy,* she kept saying, *my poor little boy, I don't understand, my baby.*

Finally she seemed to calm a little.

"Where is he?"

"In your bedroom." It was still *my bedroom.* "I locked him up in your bedroom—I don't know—last night, early this morning. It's smaller. And he just won't stop. I couldn't look at him anymore! I couldn't watch it! I tried to pad it for him. I just couldn't stop him."

"How long has this been going on, mom?"

"Since yesterday. You know he'd been bumping into things now and then because he couldn't see. But this was different. It was like he was all of a sudden *searching* for something. Something he couldn't find. And he kept walking faster and faster like he was, I don't know, desperate, banging into everything, and crying, making these terrible whimpering sounds—banging into the fireplace, my *god!* the fireplace! The chairs. But I couldn't stop him, I'd hold him for a while and I'd think I had him calmed down but then as soon as I let him go he'd start right up again. He won't eat. He hasn't eaten."

"We'll get him to the vet."

I got up and got his leash off the kitchen doorknob and walked down the hall to the bedroom. She didn't follow.

And there was Beau all right, walking directly into my closet door. Turning and lurching into one of the bedposts as though he were drunk. She'd wadded up bathtowels, sheets and blankets and even some of my old shirts for padding along the walls and furniture but he was still hitting things *hard* and I couldn't tell how much good they were doing. His muzzle was glistening.

The sounds were awful.

I picked him up and at first he tried to wriggle free but then I guess he got the scent of me and turned and licked my face. The gesture made me want to cry. Instead I sat down and patted and petted him and talked to him. *Good old boy. You gotta cut this out, you know that? We're gonna get you to the vet. Get you back to your old self again. You'll see.*

I was lying through my teeth. His heart was racing. He was ten years old, almost eleven. He'd been sustaining this kind of exertion for a day and a half.

I was amazed he'd made it this long.

I clipped the leash to his collar and carried him down the hall.

My mother still sat on the couch.

"You ready, mom?"

She stared down into her lap.

"I can't, Rob. I can't go with you. I know what the vet's going to say. And I can't do that to him. I just *can't.*" Then she was crying again, her shoulders quaking. "You understand?"

I could lie to the dog but not to her.

"Are you sure?"

"Yes. I'm sure. You go. He's your dog too. Just give him to me a for minute, will you?"

I placed him on her lap and he stayed there quietly while she stroked him.

I thought she'd want some privacy so I went into the kitchen and poured myself a glass of juice and took my time drinking it until she called me.

She'd been crying again naturally but she kissed him goodbye on top of the head and moved her hand off his back so I lifted him up and took him outside into the bright spring sunshine and put him down on the lawn and walked with him and watched him sniff around like any dog would until he found a spot near the sidewalk that suited him and watched him lift his leg and piss a trace of himself into the fresh-cut grass for some passing dog to find.

Then I lifted him into the car and drove away with one hand on the wheel and the other holding onto his collar because he kept wanting to walk again, lurching up toward the unforgiving dashboard so that I had to gently pull him down again and drove the three or four miles to the vet's office.

Everyone knew us there. Beau was a frequent visitor. The pretty dark-haired nurse took one look at him and with sweetness and concern rushed us to an examining table in a private room and went to fetch the doctor. I petted and talked to him and held him still until a few moments later Dr. Laury appeared. I filled her in on what was happening.

She touched him with care, more even than I was used to from her, wiped the blood old and new from his muzzle with a wet towel, listened to his heart and lungs and examined his eyes.

"I think he's had a stroke of the optic nerve," she said. "It's called Giant Cell Arteritis—GCA. It's caused by poor circulation to the blood vessels in the nerve. We'd have to run some bloods. And I'm afraid we'd have to do a biopsy of the temple region to be sure. I've got to be honest with you, this isn't good."

"Any treatment?"

"Not much I'm afraid. If that's what this is, there are drugs we can use to try to improve the blood-flow to the area. But he's already on blood-pressure medication, isn't he. You said he's not eating?"

"No he's not."

"And he's how old? Almost eleven?"

"Yes."

Then she just looked at me.

"He's hurting, Rob," she said. "Not just from walking into walls. His joints hurt and it probably hurts to chew. That's why he's not eating."

I thought of that dog in Greece and wondered suddenly if it wasn't pain that had turned him into a monster. I thought that it probably was. Just as simple as that. Pain of some sort. Then I thought about what my mother had said about Beau being my dog too and it was clear to me that she was right, that probably it had been true all along but I just hadn't noticed—because I didn't feed him every day, walk him every day. Maybe Aristophanes' owner had noticed I had a dog already but not me, I hadn't been looking closely enough. But there was no question that he was mine now. Mine to do the right thing by.

I think I forgave the Greek dog then and there.

Thought I understood him. Even wished him well. Because now Beau was something of a monster too—a monster to himself. Beyond all blame yet a creature defined overnight by hurt. His body forsaking the pup inside, betraying the dog my mother loved and who I loved and who loved us in return.

I realized I knew something about betrayal too. And had for quite a while.

"I want to be there," I said. "I want to hold him. Is that all right?"

"That's just fine," she said.

She saw the tears. She reached out and placed her hand gently on my forearm.

Just as I knew she would.

I held him to the end and said a soft goodbye.

From my mother's house I called Dorothy's apartment and told her what had happened. We talked for a long while. I told her that I wouldn't be coming back to New York that night, I was staying here with my mother. She was understanding and kind. At the end of it I told her I was thinking of settling in for a while, turning down some assignments, turning down a whole lot of assignments maybe, possibly even trying my hand at a book.

Who knew?

She laughed at me but I could tell she was very pleased.

"You're full of surprises," she said.

"What next? A dog?"

Thanks to William Brockett

Bill Brockett's a merchant seaman and an old buddy of mine He called me one day and said he'd just had the strangest experience. He was outside a Connecticut store doing some shopping when this great big guy, a total stranger with a great big dog came along and for some reason he was *sure* this guy was going to talk to him and then just as sure he was going to *touch* him. Brockett's not exactly a touchy-feely kind of guy nor is he particularly given to psychic intuitions but it turned out to be a very pleasant encounter. Though he worried for a while that the guy might have been a Jonah consigning him to the deep.

The incident with the dog in Mykonos is true and happened to me pretty much just as I wrote it. Same with having to put down my mom's dog, Beau.

I got some string and pulled the three together.

—JK

Consensual

by Jack Ketchum writing as Jerzy Livingston

We rolled away from one another. We were exhausted both of us but for different reasons. Her reason was that her coming had been a hell of a long time coming. So long in fact that I was practically ready to go again. They say the tongue is the strongest muscle in the body per square inch and I didn't know about that but mine felt like it had been bench-pressing hundred-pound weights.

A hundred repetitions.

"You want a beer, Stroup?" she said.

Her fingernails were drawing tight little circles around my navel. I was old enough to be her father. It didn't matter. If she kept that up I'd be ready again any minute but my tongue still needed a rest.

"A beer would be nice, Carol."

She reached across my chest for the royal blue kimono I only knew was royal blue because now and then I'd seen it in the light. She kept the bedroom as dark as the inside of a cave and at the moment it smelled about as rank.

Summertime sex in the city. I heard the rustle of silk and her perfume wafted toward me like a sudden field of clover. "Be right back," she said.

The bedroom door opened and she stepped out into the dimly lit hallway and I could see a little. The kimono fluttered across her thighs like a big grateful butterfly riding along for the nectar.

It had been three weeks now I'd been fucking Carol and I'd yet to see her wholly naked. Her habit was to turn off the lights before we started and close the bedroom door behind her like this was a quickie and she was expecting company any minute even though it wasn't a quickie and she lived alone. The blinds were always drawn. She never seemed to want to fuck in daytime so the most I could tell from what little ambient light the city streets provided was that she wasn't deformed, had a nice little mole on her left front hip and was of a generally uniform color.

I asked her once what was with the Stygian Darkness bit.

We couldn't light a candle maybe?

We'd both quit smoking. So glowing embers were out.

She laughed. "I dunno, Stroup. I think it's sort of sexy. A little spooky. Like I can't tell what you're going to do next, where you're going to touch me. A little dangerous. It's like I'm doing it with...well, a kind of succubus, you know?"

"Incubus. Succubus would be you."

"Right. You don't mind, do you?"

"To quote our president, 'Security is the essential roadblock to achieving a road map to peace.' "

"Huh?"

"Look it up. Washington, D.C., July 25th, 2003."

"I don't understand."

"Whatever makes you feel secure or insecure, Carol, whichever you want it's fine with me. Even if they're as confused as that dickless fuck. The exceptions being golden showers, vomiting on purpose and coprolagnia."

"Coprolagnia?"

"Playing with shit."

"Eeeeew."

"I thought you'd feel that way."

I'd never questioned her about it since. Though sometimes I wanted to. Taste touch and scent are perfectly good senses but sometimes you want a little presentation as well. The parsley sprig on the dinnerplate.

She slid into the room through the crack in the doorway with two cold Becks sweating in the bottle and we savored them. We'd met over Becks at the All State Café.

She asked me if I had to work tomorrow. I told her I didn't—the goddamn copy was in. *Drill bits.* I was writing about drill bits. The book was a flop everywhere but at the remainder tables so I was back to copy again. My next assignment? Crest Whitestrips. Don't be annoyed if you can't quite see the connection.

"You?"

"No. I switched shifts with Janet."

That was a relief. I didn't need the guilt. It was two in the morning already. Carol was a nurse's aide on the geriatric ward over at St. Luke's and even though she was twenty-five years younger than me, still a just kid as far as I was concerned, even on a good day with plenty of sleep she was dead on her feet half the time when it was over.

"That mean we can go again?"

She smiled and finished her beer. "Mmmmm," she said. "Sure does."

She set the beer down and got up and closed the door.

Closing the door. That was how I knew she was serious.

The dark descended and she descended spread-legged across my thighs a few seconds later. She was naked. No kimono. Her body was cool to the touch and then it wasn't.

We made the usual noises.

"You know what we never do, Stroup?" she said.

She was riding me high, posting like a rider in an equestrian event and I was below her pumping away. I wasn't really used to questions at this juncture.

"Uh, what?"

"We don't talk about what we like. About what really gets us off."

"I thought we were getting off pretty good, Carol."

"We are."

For emphasis she hit the saddle, twice. Hit it *hard*. Think a pair of body blows from Sonny Liston.

The saddle said *"OH!"* and *"OH!"* The saddle was way too old for this shit.

She posted again. Much better.

"What I mean is, everybody has some special thing or things they like during sex, right? Sometimes you find out what they are by accident, trial and error. You trip over them. But it's better to just tell it, get it out there, don't you think? Because sometimes the person never finds out."

"Kind of like a g-spot?" I said. "A sort of little-to-the-left kind of thing?"

"Kind of. What do you like, Stroup?"

"I like this, Carol."

"I know you do. You're not going to come yet are you?"

"Not if we keep talking. I don't think so."

"Good."

I wasn't exactly sure I was telling the truth. It was a pretty safe bet that Carol wouldn't come even with me working her clit with thumb and forefinger which I'd been doing continually since she climbed aboard with only that one minor pause during her switch from equestrian to bronc buster. The noises she made told me she liked that fine but it was the tongue that really got to her in general. The weightlifter.

"So what do you really like? Tell me and I'll do it."

"I'm embarrassed, Carol..."

"No you're not. Nothing embarrasses you."

"Our president does."

"Bush aside, Stroup."

"That didn't sound right. Not under these circumstances. Was that meant to be instructional? You want to rephrase that?"

"Goddamn President Bush aside, Stroup."

"My nipples are sensitive."

"What? Right now? Is that a bad thing?"

"No. The left one slightly more so than the right. You sort of nibble at it that'd be good. But either one will do. Left or right. Your pick."

"I thought it was only women who were really sensitive there. That's rare in guys, isn't it, Stroup?"

"I don't know. It's not the sort of thing that normally comes up in conversation during the Yankee game. 'You see that line drive? Yeah! Man! My nipples are sensitive!'"

Then I shut up because she bent over and went to work on the left one and she was so obviously a natural at it that I had to wonder if there wasn't a woman in her past somewhere, thinking it was maybe something to ask her about later not that I minded one way or another and I could feel it travel all the way down my spine into my cock in little electric bursts. She must have sensed something because she pulled away.

"You going to come, Stroup?"

"Mmmmmuhhhhh," I said.

"Oh no you're not."

And I didn't even see it coming. There was no way to roll with the thing. It was a good one too. All of a sudden my cheek was burning and the crown on my molar, upper right quadrant, felt loose.

"Jesus, Carol! You slapped me! You goddamn *slapped* me!"

I had to admit it had done the trick though. I was down. Though not out.

"Sorry. Reach over and turn on the light, Stroup."

"Huh?"

"I want to show you something. The table lamp. Turn it on."

This was interesting.

I was going to see whatever it was she hadn't wanted me to see so far.

At first I couldn't figure it. She looked like a woman with all parts intact. Very much intact—and I wondered for the umpteenth time what she saw in an old bum like me. Her areolae were darker than I'd expected. The navel dove deeper than my tongue had bothered to notice. That was about it.

She turned a little to the right and I saw the white smooth scar tissue over two of her left ribs, crawling toward her back a few inches below her breast. The one on top was maybe an inch long. The one below it more like three.

"Whew," I said. "And I never felt those?"

"I hold my elbow this way, it's hard to reach them. See? Do they disgust you?"

"Hell no, Carol. Guys like scars. We're kinda odd that way. But what the hell happened?"

I pumped a few times and she posted just to keep things rolling.

"I was driving my boyfriend's car one night back in high school. Some drunk kissed my bumper passing me on Route 10 and I went off an embankment. My boyfriend was so goddamn proud of that car—vintage black '71 Volvo, in fabulous condition. But there were no airbags back then and I wasn't wearing a belt so I went into the steering wheel. Compound fracture of the ribs. I reached around and I could feel them sticking out of me. It was pretty...intense."

"Intense? I would think so. God, yes."

"I came like a sonovabitch, Stroup."

"What?"

"I swear to god. I didn't think it was ever going to stop. It was *pouring* out of me"

"This is a joke now, right?"

"No. It was pretty embarrassing too. I was wearing these Garfield THRILL ME panties and they were just soaked through completely. And you know, the medics, they had to undress me, so..."

She let it just trail off that way. That was fine by me. I was starting to wilt again.

She pumped. I pumped. That was better.

But I was starting to get this feeling. This weird, bad association. I had the sense that what she was going to say to me next would not be about nipple nibbling or blowing in her ear.

"I get off on broken bones, Stroup. That's my thing."

"You do. You get off on broken bones."

"I do. For me there's nothing like it."

"That's pretty new and different, Carol."

"I know. But I'm not the only one, Stroup. There are chat groups on the net. There's websites."

"Uh-huh."

"You should check it out."

"Sure. Why not? I've already been through most of the quadruple-amputee sites."

"I'm serious, Stroup."

"I'm sorry. I didn't mean any offense, Carol. Honest."

"So will you?"

"What? Break your ribs?"

She laughed. "No, silly. That would be getting pretty extreme, don't you think? You could do a finger, though. I'd really like that. In fact I'm getting all hot just thinking about you breaking my finger, Stroup. Will you do that for me?"

"I wouldn't know how, for godsakes. What if I tried to break it and just disjointed it or something? Would that be disappointing to you?"

"You think I'm crazy, don't you."

"No. I think you're getting wetter all the time, though. Jeez."

"I told you. I work with osteoporosis patients, Stroup, you know? They break bones every day. Sometimes I get so hot I have to go to the ladies' room and... am I telling you too much about this?"

"It's possible."

"You think I'm crazy."

"I do not. If you wanted to get pregnant that would be crazy."

"Fuck me, Stroup. Break my finger, okay?"

"I..."

"How isn't a problem. I'll show you how."

"You've done this before."

"Not to myself. It doesn't work if I try to do it. I chicken out. Somebody else has to. But yeah, there have been guys willing. Look at this."

She swung her left foot up beside me on the bed. I thought that was pretty damn athletic of her. I pumped a few times. New position. Not bad.

"See that?"

Her big toe was a mess. All bent to hell out of shape. I hadn't noticed that. Who looks at feet?

"That was Ron. He went overboard one night with a pair of pliers. I told the doctors a manhole cover fell on it. I don't think they believed me, though. I dumped him the following day."

She swung the leg around. We were in post position again. She pulled up high so that I was almost out of her. Almost but not quite. My shaft was suddenly very cool and wet. The glans nestled.

"Here's what you do," she said.

She took the pinkie of her left hand between the thumb and forefinger of her right so that the thumb pressed flat against the bottom of the second joint and the forefinger pressed down over the knuckle.

"This is called a phalanx. It's a very small bone but you'd be surprised how hard it is to break. See, the joint ligaments and capsule tend to rupture before the bone snaps. Which is pretty intense too but it's not what we're after here. You have to do it fast and you only get one try."

She drew up and down, up and down. A smile in her eyes and on her lips.

"C'mon, Stroup," she said. "Astound me."

I took her hand. I placed my fingers just so.

I guess I got it right.

"You know, not many guys will do this, Stroup."

"I'm not surprised."

She moved aside the heavy butcher-block cutting board and snuggled close. It was the following night. I had just taken out her terminal phalanx—the tip of her pinkie—with a ball peen hammer. Smashed it against the board.

Same hand.

The board was wet with blood. The bed was wet with us.

She'd decided to wait on dealing with the first break—just splinted it herself. She was going in to work tomorrow and she'd have both of them taken care of then. She hadn't decided on the right explanation yet.

I couldn't help her on that one. My imagination failed me.

Meantime she'd thought ahead this time and had gauze and tape and peroxide and codeine waiting on the nightstand. At least I didn't have to look at the thing. Unless you counted seepage.

"How bad is it?"

She smiled. "Bad. I took the codeine, though. I really want you to know, Stroup. That was one of the best. God, that was good!"

"Thanks. You weren't so bad yourself. What next?"

She considered. "I dunno. I work with my hands. So I have to give these time to heal. A toe, maybe?"

"You'll limp."

"I bought these shoes that are a little too big, you know? Just in case."

"In case?

"In case I met somebody like you, Stroup."

I couldn't fathom what in the hell it was she was feeling. Imagination failed me there too. She seemed happy though.

"Yeah. Toes, I think," she said.

"Plural?"

"One to start with, silly. I've got this vise under the bed in the toolbox. You can do it slowly. Little by little. Oh my god, Stroup, there I go, I'm getting wet again!"

"Wait a minute. You're not saying...?"

"No, jesus, I couldn't take that now. Not after this."

"Okay. I get it. You got it. I'm there."

I slid down the long delicious length of her and proceeded.

I mashed her middle toe, right foot, the following week.

It occurred to me that Carol might have done very well during the Inquisition. *Thumbscrews, The Boot, The Rack.* I doubt they'd have known what to make of her though except to be terrified out of their freaking minds that they'd actually finally *met* a witch and would've burned her first chance they got. That would have been the downside I guess. Carol wasn't into burning.

I'd asked her.

If they noticed the limp at work nobody said anything.

She had some vacation days coming so I took some time off from the ad copy and we flew to Sarasota. The agency was pissed. They wanted me to do a TV-only ad for a Best of Barry Manilow collection. You know the type. Your CD starts skipping before you hit the PLAY button. I told them I was wrong for the job anyway. I liked heavy metal. They said there was evidence heavy metal was turning kids into murderers. I told them if that was true then Barry Manilow was probably turning them into florists.

It was the beginning of May so the Florida humidity hadn't descended yet and the hotel was cheap enough so we rented a car and spent the days basking in the sun on the fine white sand at Siesta Key and window shopping at St. Armand's Circle, eating streetside there and then going back to our hotel to do what we did best together and it was only when she showed me the Louisville Slugger that I got worried.

We were lying in bed. Mr. Muscle was very sore.

"Correct me if I'm wrong but isn't that assault and battery? No pun intended."

"Not if it's consensual. I figure if you choke up high on it you can bring it down right over my forearm."

"Both hands?"

"I think you'd have to use both hands, yeah. Otherwise it's not gonna break. I'll just wind up with a hell of a bruise."

"And we don't want that."

"No."

"Can I think about it?"

"Sure. I'm too pooped tonight away. I just thought, how appropriate, you know? We're here in Sarasota. The Cincinnati Reds do their spring training down here. Whenever I see them on TV I'll think of you."

I was dead tired too but I kept thinking lying there in bed that I was maybe getting in a little over my head on this and that the pinkie or toe were one thing but that the radius or ulna were probably another. Not to mention all the sensitive nerves and tender blood vessels in attendance. That I could possibly cripple the nutty bitch and then where would I be? My sleep was troubled. I remember morphing into Yogi Berra at some point and that Berra was striking out again—he could never hit worth a damn—and I remember thinking the way you do when you're half asleep and half awake that I wasn't even playing for the right team.

At another point I was arrested by the Sarasota police.

The charge was breaking and entering.

The wake-up call was good though. The wake up call was Carol's lips sliding up and down my dick and before you could say Boy Howdy I was tickling her tonsils with the thing.

She looked up and smiled around it and I think she said *"morning."*

I know I said morning back.

She lifted herself up onto her knees and slid me inside her and started moving back and forth and side to side and soon I was starting to come, I could tell it was on its way not only from the feeling down below but because I have this sort of involuntary grunting moaning thing I do way back in my throat—and because I had my eyes closed I didn't see it coming a second time.

She'd reached down behind her on the bed I guess and next thing I knew my right collarbone felt like it had just exploded. I screamed and bucked her off me back hard onto my thighs and the bat flew out of her hands to the floor and my come whipped off into her hair like strands of gooey tinsel on a Christmas tree. She was smiling. I was shouting, groaning.

"You fucking...!"

"I thought you'd like to see what it was like," she said. "So, what do you think?"

"You fucking... you *crazy...fucking...*!"

And I don't know how I managed it through the pain or even saw her clearly enough through the dots of yellow bursting in front of my eyes but I leaned up into her and planted my left fist into the side of her jaw like it was born to be there once, just once in a goddamn lifetime and then leave its mark forever.

She didn't fall off the bed—she *dove* off the bed. Sideways, almost gracefully. She looked like a girl sliding dreamlike off her ski in some Esther Williams movie. Well, we were in Florida.

My collarbone was killing me. My fist was killing me. I felt like one big sack of pain.

So much for the thrill of broken bones.

Thanks so much for sharing.

I could hear her sobbing down beside the bed.

Somehow I got to my feet and walked over. She was lying on her back, her right shoulder off at a strange unnatural angle. She was trying to hold her jaw in place with her left hand.

"I think you broke my jaw," she sobbed.

At least I think that's what she said.

I could see she'd dislocated her shoulder.

I hated to watch a woman cry so I went into the bathroom and got her a hand-towel and bent down and gave it to her. That jaw looked broken all right.

"I got one question for you, Carol," I said.

I could see our near future then clear as the Sarasota night. The hospital, the explanations, probably the cops. The flight back to New York with the passengers and flight attendants all looking at us like gee, what a terrible awful shame, it must have been an awful wreck. I wonder if anybody else survived? Then the breakup, the tears, the inevitable parting of ways.

"Whussat?" she said. I had to ask.

"Didja come?"

For those of you new to Stroup he's the subject of some half a dozen wacky yarns of mine first published in men's mags during the 70s, then collected in *Broken on the Wheel of Sex*—and the hero of "Sheep Meadow Story" from the *Triage* novella anthology I did with Edward Lee and Richard Laymon. I invented him in 1976 for a story in *Swank*—in an obvious nod to Charles Bukowski—and he's been rampaging through my consciousness every now and then like some outraged misogynist bull-in-a-china-shop ever since.

I tripped over this broken-bones fetish while cruising some of the more questionable roads along the internet and decided it would be perfect for a loser like Stroup to encounter somebody of this particular bent and thought it okay and proper to unleash him again. Nanci Kalanta had asked me for a piece for Horrorworld Online and liked the story very much but said that it seemed that the only thing which outraged her readers at all seemed to be explicit sex. Not explicit horrors—gougings, dismemberments, the won-ton (wanton?) display of internal organs—but sex.

Doncha just *love* the twenty-first century?

—JK

Seascape

He rose slowly to a dim pale wavering light, crawling up through dense viscous fluid into full brightness and then finally clarity. He saw where he'd been swimming to and gasped and screamed.

"I'm going with you," she said.

He smiled and put down his crossword puzzle on the comforter beside him on the bed.

Outside the open window he could hear the sea, breakers against the jetty buffeted by winter winds.

"I don't think so. What's a five-letter word for *mooed? Moo* as in cow. Beginning with an 'L' I think."

She was polishing the bedside table, rubbing in lemon oil. *Giving it a drink* was how she put it. *"Lowed.* And who says I'm giving you a choice, Ben." She glanced at him and nodded. "Write it in," she said.

Charlie Harmon had just passed by with a linen cart when he heard the scream devolve into a long low moan streaming out from 314 and he moved past the uniformed cop peering in through the doorway, brushed his shoulder as he passed so that the cop seemed to glare at him a moment and it was only once he'd reached the old man's bed that Charlie realized the cop was only startled—and maybe even a little scared.

The nurse was Denise. One of the good ones. Denise had brains and dedication and her voice had the ability to soothe without false cheer. She was using it on him now as she lifted his head gently off the pillow and firmed it under him and set him back down again and then reached for a tissue on the bedstand and dabbed his eyes. *You just take it easy now you been through an a lot Mr. Sebald you just*

*rest up and you're gonna be fine, doctor'll be in here soon and I'll be right
back I'm just going to get you a little chipped ice for your throat okay? And
you need anything else either Charles here or I'll come runnin' won't we
Charles.*

Outside in the hall again he walked with her to the nurses'
station and the ice machine and she sighed and shook her head.

"I don't know," she said. "Sometimes I just don't understand."

"What's with the cop?" Charlie said.

The ice tumbled down into the plastic cup.

"Suicide watch," she said.

There was never a time in memory when Ben hadn't loved the sea.
Summers when he and his older brother John were growing up his
family had rented a small wind-battered bungalow in Asbury Park,
New Jersey—long before the town's slide into decay—the same place
five years running.

The house lay directly on the beach. The porch was always
dusted and sometimes halfway-buried with sand. A boy could roll
out of bed and grab a glass of orange juice and a piece of buttered
toast and five minutes later be scouting the hard wet tideline for
horseshoe crabs and jellyfish marooned along the shore.

At high tide he bodysurfed the whitecaps tumbling to the beach.

He took part-time jobs summers during his college years at a
lumberyard in Cape Cod and a greasy-spoon diner in Falmouth
just to be near the sea and the kind of life the sea afforded—so long
as you didn't have to buck it for a living. A life of flesh and youth.
Of tan-lines and dried white jagged salt lines against the skin, skin
that glowed at night in driftwood firelight, that flaked and peeled
and just below which lay a smooth new layer, fresh pink and
incorruptible. He met his future wife Ruth—just twenty years old
then—over lobster and corn on the cob at a clambake on the beach
one night a few miles north of Portland, Maine

They slept together in the gentle susurration of that same beach
the following night and with no one else ever again.

When his brother John died he and Ruth had been living in
New York City for almost thirty years. But the sea had never lost
its lure for John either. Quite the contrary. He'd bought a small cape
codder and set up practice directly after medical school in what was

then the sleepy little town of Cape May, New Jersey long before the tourists discovered its turn-of-the-century charm—a house down by the Point where his only neighbor was a nun's retreat, St. Mary's by the Sea. When his heart failed him lunchtime one hot late-August afternoon walking out of the air-conditioned Ugly Mug into the sticky thick humidity along the sidewalk he had just turned sixty. He had never married. He left the house to Ben and Ruth.

They'd been happy in New York but there was nothing particularly keeping them there. Ruth had retired from the bank two years before and Ben's illustration work came and went by mail. They had no children and two tabby cats, George and Gracie, who were only too happy to be packed up and moved to someplace where birds large and small swooped by all day long or pecked around for bugs along the porch, where bees and dragonflies zoomed and darted into view and moths fluttered nightly at the windowpanes.

They had all but stopped making love in the City.

The seashore was their fountain of youth.

"How's your Shakespeare these days?' she said.

"What?"

"Your Shakespeare. Put your puzzle down again."

"Okay."

" *'If it be a sin to covet honor, I am the most offending soul alive.'* "

"That's Henry something."

"That's right. The Fifth. The St. Crispin's Day speech. Very good. Now listen to me. I not only love you, I *honor* you. Are you listening? Yes? Good. And you honor me, right?"

"Yes."

"Then don't argue, dammit. The cats can stay with my sister. She adores them."

The shivering came in waves and it was violent, as though he were trying to shake himself apart and not what Ryan knew he was really doing, generating heat. But the pauses between episodes of shivering got longer and longer as they undressed and dried him down and then wrapped him in the polypropylene and woolen blankets and the space blankets, applied the chemical heat packs to his neck, his armpits, his groin and the palms of his hands yet finally, despite all that, the shivering had stopped altogether and now Ryan was worried as hell. Because now there was no radial pulse and only the faintest in the carotid. And that looked to be winding down as well.

They hoisted the stretcher into the rear. They were doing it by the book but the man was slipping. His temperature was down to 86 degrees and he was damn slow about getting it up any further.

He was looking at a guy whose body had passed through hibernation into a state of metabolic icebox here. Blue skin, muscles rigid, pupils fixed and no discernible2 breathing. He looked dead. He acted dead. But Ryan knew he wasn't dead and wouldn't be for a while at least. They played possum on you. The rule of thumb with victims of hypothermia was that there was no such thing as cold and dead. Only *warm and dead.*

He shut the doors behind them. The heating unit was already blasting.

His partner Knowles had the warm dextrose drip into him and they were feeding him warm moist oxygen. Outer temperature was important against further heat-loss but not nearly as important as internal. They had to stabilize and try to raise his core temp as soon as possible or they were looking at potential damage to the heart, lungs or brain. Or all three put together.

"CPR?" said Knowles.

"No way. He's still got a pulse. We stay with that for now. At this point his heart's hyperexcitable as hell. We do CPR and he's still pulsing we risk arrhythmia. We could kill the poor bastard."

"Okay. What then?"

He heard an engine rev and glanced out the double doors and saw their sister EV pull away awkwardly across the sand.

"Relieve him. That's what we do," he said. "I want to express his urine. He's got a bladder big as a football from cold dieresis and he's using up heat to keep *that* warm instead of the rest of him. There are times our bodies aren't too swift about priorities."

"We ready to roll yet, gentlemen?" said Andrews from the front seat. Andrews was young and way too impatient for his own good but he was a damn good driver.

"One second," Ryan said. "Knowles, grab me a Foley twelve.

Our guy's gotta see a man about a horse."

He held out his hand for the catheter.

The first thing he learned about even the possibility of being seriously ill was how lonely it was.

It was lonely to its very core. People could be concerned, kind, encouraging and even loving but illness was a thing you did all on your own—something no outside hand could touch. Certainly not the doctors. The doctors were there simply in the capacity of benign detectives. Well, hopefully benign at least. To them you were a sort of crossword puzzle to be either solved or abandoned as impossible to solve whatever the case may be. Later they might rise to the level of trusted advisors. Still later, once you damn well knew you *were* sick, angels, demons, or secular gods.

Yet even in their hands as they poked and prodded you were alone, cast deep inside yourself. Aware finally that the flesh which had once sustained you beyond any question or second of doubt was now unexpectedly falling prey to time and dissolution. That your flesh had now turned undependable—and in Ben's case, since it was prostate cancer and metastasizing like crazy—that it had turned into the enemy, was hard to explain even to yourself. Incomprehensible to anyone else.

It was your flesh and thus your personal enemy and yours alone. The word *alone* had never held such clarity and weight.

A caress could comfort. Sure. But it couldn't pay the troops enough to convince them to continue the battle. The troops were tired. The troops were all in mutiny.

Ruth had tried of course.

She suffered too—from osteoporosis. And osteoporosis was pain in spades god knows and a betrayal all its own but people lived for years with it. It wasn't a hangman's noose waiting in the yard.

"Remember?"

Her single counterinsurgency weapon was their past and she wielded it tenderly and with grace.

Remember? The antique store in England where they bought the cedar chest. the owner right out of Dickens. The climb to the shrine at Delos where the wind took her wide-brim hat and sailed it out to sea. Setting up his first painters' studio in Portland and not a job coming in for months,

Ben painting angry frustrated abstracts until finally Bantam came through with the fantasy series. He should have stayed with the abstracts, she said, which were selling in the high five figures. Their first kitten, Agamemnon, who had hidden sulking under the bed for a week like Achilles in his tent and then suddenly for no observable reason decided that he was master of all he surveyed. High tea with Liz and Josie at the Plaza. Christmas dinner with Neil and Donald on Mount Desert Island. On and on.

Her version of events was not always as he remembered them but he supposed that was to be expected.

And that was the second thing he learned about being seriously ill.

What a strange and special repository he was.

How much sheer history you had inside you that was going to die when you did.

He realized with a kind of growing awe that his own version of events would simply disappear shortly as though it had never existed. What would be left would be Ruth's version, or friends' or relatives' versions, or his publishers' versions. His own point of view, that which was uniquely Ben Sebald's, would pass utterly from the world's vocabulary. And his secrets—guilty personal failings which he had tried to keep hidden from everyone all these years, even from Ruth—would ironically become irrelevant. As perhaps they always were anyway.

He told her what he wanted to do.

"What about Greece?" she said. "You always loved Greece."

"Not Greece this time."

"I'm going with you."

"I don't think so. What's a five-letter word for *mooed*?"

Charlie Harmon was on lunch break in the Caféteria and his luck was bad again. Sorenson sat down unwelcome as always with his tray directly across from him and the tuna salad on his plate was about the same color and seemingly the same texture as Sorenson's teeth. His brilliant hospital whites only enhanced the illusion. Charlie's appetite was rapidly swimming downstream.

"True story," Sorenson said. "We had three drunks in here from Wildwood one night couple years ago. Tail-end of a very liquid wedding party. I mean, they're loaded as hell. So they decide to jump off the pier together. Made a pact. Said they'd had it—enough's enough, right? Life sucks. Maybe they couldn't get laid that night, who the fuck knows. But see, one of them's wearing this really expensive cashmere coat and he takes it off and puts it down on the rocks and on their way off the pier arm in arm one of the other drunks steps on it. The guy with the coat says, you fucking piece of shit! Why'd you step on my coat? Why the fuck would I want to go out with an inconsiderate piece of shit like you? And he starts swinging. The third guy, their buddy, he gets between the two of them and before you know it all three of these guys are in the drink and not one of them can fucking swim. They were lucky the groom came down for a smoke. His wife didn't care for cigarettes."

Charlie looked at him.

"So your point is?"

Sorenson shrugged. "No point, Charlie. Just how fucked up is this business anyway though, huh? Just how fucked up is it?"

"Jesus" Harmon said. "Eat your lunch."

He held her as he always had when they were young. His arms still strong around her back as he kissed her and then shifted his weight suddenly and toppled them off the jetty into the blaze of freezing water—black granite and weathered lichen-covered concrete already well beyond their grasp in just an instant's time should they even have thought to reach for it again as the swells moved them back and forth to sea. She gasped at the sudden blinding cold and clutched his waist.

The tide went wild only once and threw him back amid spray and foam into one of the huge granite blocks beneath the surface bruising his hip just below where the ropes bound the two of them together and then sent them floating free.

They went down and then up again and he could feel them shivering almost in a kind of unison and her eyes were wide blinking away the water and her face had taken on an unlikely pallor. *I love you* he shouted and she began to say the same I love...when they were drawn down beneath a wave. When they rose again he shook his head and realized in that movement of his neck how much his muscles were already stiffening. *This soon*, he thought. *Good*. His throat felt rubbed with salt. The membranes in his nostrils burned.

His eyes burned too but he could still blink the sting away and look at her. At some version of her anyhow, one he had never quite seen before whose lips and eyelids were stained a delicate blue. With a shock he saw that she was smiling. Or perhaps the muscles of her face were contracting into what appeared to be a smile—perhaps it was a swindle of a smile. But he didn't think so. He thought that it was real. He felt light-headed, almost drunk himself. He pulled her closer until he couldn't feel his hands anymore and then his arms around her and when finally the sea drew him down to darkness he wasn't sure exactly who was there with him at all.

When Ryan, Knowles and Andrews responded to the call and pulled up beside the old man on the beach he still had the rope lashed around his waist but the other end had come free so that their sister unit found the woman several yards away lying face-down just above the tideline with her head half buried in the hard wet sand. The two kids who'd found them couldn't have been more than ten years old but that didn't stop one of them from having a cell phone. Times like this you could almost like the goddamn things. It had maybe saved the guy.

From what Ryan could tell the woman wasn't likely to make it.

She had eaten a lot of sand.

He woke and saw where he'd been swimming to and that he was alone.

He gasped and screamed.

"You're a fool," she said quieting him. *"I love you but you're a very foolish man, you know that? I know you. What you'll do is, you'll wait a few months. And you'll just agonize all that time. All that awful time. With the cancer and about me too. When you don't have to. You can come right now. Just as we'd planned. You just start swimming again. You know the tides."*

"Aw, *goddammit!*" said Charlie Harmon. "*Shit!*" He reached for the paddles and thrust them at her. "God*dammit!*"

"Hush," said Denise. "Charlie, look at his face. Look at him. You see that?"

He looked down at the man and then at her.

Her dark green eyes were pooled and still.
"Hush, Charlie," she said. "Shhhhhhh."

Thanks to Neal McPheeters and Dale Meyers Cooper,
painters with stories.

"Seascape" was generated by a clipping Neal McPheeters sent me about an old married couple who had jumped into the sea together because they couldn't bear to be parted. He was dying, while she was not—but it was she who drowned while her husband was left to die alone. I thought the story was fraught with the kinds of real everyday horrors and awful ironies that life sometimes dishes up for us.

Because the tale was basically such a simple one I chose a structure which would jump-cut back and forth in time in order to conceal somewhat exactly where it was going and give it the heft and impact I thought it needed. I changed its locale to Cape May, New Jersey because I know Cape May—Neal and his wife Victoria live there—and resolved to give it a strangely happy romantic ending.

I also thought it needed at least one brief moment of comic relief so I included the yarn about the drunken suicide pact and the cashmere coat. Another fine painter, Dale Meyers Cooper, told me that one. And she swears it's true.

—JK

Snarl, Hiss, Spit, Stalk

Dead cat bored dead.
All dead boring. Mayflies, wallabies, Hottentots. Everything.
Dead cat boring self.
Same old same old.
Dead cat take a shot at living again. Can't hurt.

Easy this time.
Dead cat borrow love from crazy human. Human slash her wrists for love of lover.
Crazy human cry and mumble. Disgusting, weak, pathetic.
Too chicken to bounce.
Dead cat not chicken.
Dead cat cat.
Dead cat bounce.

Love confusing, heavy. Hard to carry. Hate a whole lot easier.
Hate direct, simple
Love a lot like chasing birds. Cat leap, bird flies. Cat fall. Dead cat heavy.
Pow.

Love take cat many places. Interesting.
Closet. Dark and smelly. Nap.
Pillow. Soft. Nap.
Microwave. Hard, buzzing sound, beeping sound.
Whatever. Nap.
Bookshelf. Way way up. Nap.
Box. Cardboard. Smells good. Nap.

Lap. Nap.
Lap?
Cat is where, exactly?

Human. Woman. Asleep on couch in human dwelling. Why not cat on couch? Couch soft, warm. Why on woman? Not remember journey.
Love confusing, heavy.
Woman's hand heavy. A little. Not bad.
Woman warm. Woman breathe. Belly in and out. Rhythm soothing. Long long time since Dead cat breathe. Lap warm. Hand warm. Not bad.
Dead cat stay awhile.

Dead cat make odd sound. Can't help it.
Remember it from somewhere.
Dead cat purring.

Dead cat curious, explore environment. Woman still sleeping. Slip out from under. Easy.
Environment small, three squares, twelve corners. Three doors. Floor, ceiling. In two squares dripping water. Nooks in bookshelves cat can get into. Closet cat can get into. Bed cat can sit on or hide under. Cabinet cat can get into.
If cat cares to.

Windows. Light. Humans below on street. Birds. More humans. Humans with dogs. None with cats—dead or otherwise. *Many* humans. Some walking. Some in small rolling environments. Environments moving fast. Birds afraid.
No wonder.

Dead cat jump in tub. Dead crazy woman slashed wrists in tub. Why? Why here? Smooth, cold. Not interesting. Dead cat jump out again, up by dripping water. Dripping water more interesting. Slightly.
Dead cat look in mirror. Mirror *very* interesting. Ugly cat look back. Rags, wrappings. Fur a mess. Matted, caked, dirty.

Dead cat try to spruce up a bit. Tear away wrappings. Use tongue on fur. Hard work. Neck sore, tongue sore. Cat not sure why cat doing this. Like love, confusing.

Finished.
Almost look like live cat now.
Almost.

Hear sound.
Door open. Door shut. Shut loud.
Hear man's voice, woman's voice. Man loud. Man angry. Woman scared.
Dead cat jump down and peer around corner. Sniff the air. Man smell funny. Like old meat. Man unsteady. Two big feet not enough for man. Needs four. Maybe then steady.
Big man loud.
Woman step back to wall. Cat step forward. Curious.
Dead cat *look inside* big man. Easy.
Not pretty.
Gift of hate. Empty. Live man dead inside already.
Matter of time
Woman different. Soft. Scared. Alive.
Dead cat curious. This interesting. Dead and live together, shouting. Confusing.
Dead cat step into room. Ears alert, nose alert, tail alert, cautious.
Man see cat. Point to cat and yell at woman. Yell loud. All man does is yell. Big man boring. Woman see cat. Shake her head at man. Woman confused.
Cat from nowhere. No wonder.

Man slap woman. Slap again. Slap again. Woman cry, fall to floor. Hands on face.
Man walk to cat and try to kick.
Dead cat faster.
Bounce off wall and land and snarl. Bristle fur, arch back. Bare teeth. Hiss. Man more interesting now. Man afraid. Dead cat stalk man slow across the floor. Great big man-prey chicken.
Cat not chicken. Cat cat.

Jump or not jump?

Jump!

Dead cat climb man thigh to shoulder. Fast. Easy.
Fun.
Man scream, grab Dead cat. Dead cat cling to man, forelegs to
shoulder and rear legs to belly, rear legs strong, rip, tear, claws in
manflesh deep. Stare into chicken-man's face.
Reach up. Bite man's nose. Bite good. Bite hard, draw blood. Taste
blood. Blood taste good. Man screaming loud now. That good too.

Let go. Fall to floor.
Watch man run.
Lick lips. Yum.

Hear door slam.
Silence. Woman sobbing. Dead cat trot over, rub leg.
Nuzzle. Rub other leg. Nuzzle.
Making odd sound again. Can't help it.
Give woman love, a little. Plenty left.
Love heavy, confusing. Glad to be rid of some.
Wheredidyoucomefrom? woman says.
Name? *Wheredidyoucomefrom?* Maybe.
Long name.

Woman smiling, wiping eye-water. Stroking.
Good Dead Cat spruced up a bit.
Fun.

Woman feed Dead Cat dead tuna. Not hungry. Eat anyway. Give cat
water. Not thirsty. Drink anyway.
Woman put box on bed, woman open it. Cat jump in. Not cardboard.
Cow. Smells good. Cat scratches. Feels good.
Nononoyoucan'tgointhere, woman says.
Name? *Nononoyoucan'tgointhere?* Maybe.
Very long name.

Dead cat sit, watch. Woman open drawer, put things from drawer in cow box. Drawer cat could get into. If cat wanted.

Woman sad, not crazy. Not go near the bathtub. Sad, filling box. Sad when box filled, closed, snick. Cat watch.

Woman walk to closet, reach up, take out second box. Put second box on bed. Smaller box. Holes in top. Holes in sides. Metal door all holes. Broken? No. Woman open metal door. Dead cat walk over. Sniff. Smell of live cat, long ago. No cat there though. Dead cat checked.

Thisusedtobelongtomyoldcatsonya, Ialways meanttogetanother, woman says. Name? No. Too long. Even humans not that stupid.

Box Dead Cat could get into. If cat wanted.

Dead Cat wants to.

Whatasmartkitty, woman says. *Comeonwe'regettingoutofhere.* Dead cat give her love. A little. Glad to be rid of some.

Worry about name later.

Dead cat move to place with sun, trees, grass, spiders, bees, snakes, birds, turtles, frogs, moths, fireflies, live cats, dogs.

Too many dogs. Otherwise fine.

House. Plenty places to hide. Plenty places to nap. Dead Cat still like lap though. Not bad.

Dead Cat have a name now. *Beastie.*

A little like Bastet. Otherwise fine.

Man show up.

Once. Dead Cat snarl, hiss, spit, stalk.

Man not show up after that. Ever.

Dead Cat watch. Watch woman grow older, old.

Dead Cat not grow older. Dead Cat dead.

Dead Cat give woman love, little at a time.

Stroke. Purr

Fun.

Love grow lighter, less confusing.

Dead Cat figure, good bounce.

You can't swing a dead cat in my neighborhood without hitting a Starbucks, a Citibank cash machine or a double-wide stroller but a *Swinging Cat's* another matter. Not many of those fellas around anymore. So when Gerard Houarner and Gak—two very Cool Cats indeed—asked me to re-reinvent one for an anthology called *Dead Cats Bouncing,* a companion volume to their way original *Dead Cats Bounce,* I pounced.

I tried very hard to copy Gerard's funny, quirky prose style in the story—writing in the present tense, eliminating passive verbs and prepositions, limiting adjectives and adverbs to a bare spare minimum and often stringing one-word sentences together pretty much to the goddamn breaking point.

It was an exercise in literary discipline and downright forgery I'd not attempted since trying to copy Robert Bloch's wisecracking dark-hipster voice in the seventh grade.

I had a ball.

—JK

Closing Time

Lay upon the sinner his sin,
Lay upon the transgressor his transgression...
*   —Epic of Gilgamesh*

Only the dead have seen the end of war.
                                       —Plato

OCTOBER 2001

ONE

Lenny saw the guy in his rearview mirror, the guy running toward him trying to wave him down at the stoplight, running hard, looking scared, a guy on the tall side and thin in a shiny blue insulated parka slightly too heavy for the weather—one seriously distressed individual. Probably that was because of the other beefy citizen in his shirtsleeves chasing him up 10th Avenue.

Pick him up or what?

Traffic was light. Pitifully light ever since World Trade Center a month ago. New York was nothing like it used to be traffic-wise. And it was late, half past one at night. He had the green now. Nobody ahead of him. No problem just to pull away.

And suppose he did. What was the guy gonna do? Report him to the Taxi and Limousine Commission?

You had to figure that a chase meant trouble. For sure the guy in his shirtsleeves meant trouble if he ever caught up to the poor sonovabitch. You could read the weather on his face and it was Stormy Monday all the way down the line.

Get the hell out of here, he thought. *You got a wife and kids. Don't be stupid.* 10th and 59th was usually a pretty safe place to be these days but you never could tell. Not in this town. You've been driving for nearly thirty years now. You know better. So what if he's white, middle-class. So what if you need the fare.

He lifted his foot off the brake but he'd hesitated and by then the guy was already at the door. He flung it open and jumped inside and slammed it shut again.

"Please!" he said. *"That guy back there...his goddamn wife...jesus!"*

Lenny smiled. "I got it."

He glanced at the American flag on his dashboard and thought, *I love this fucking town.*

The beefy citizen was nearly on them, coming down off the curb just a couple steps away.

Lenny floored it.

They slid uptown through time-coordinated greens like a knife through warm butter.

"Where to?"

"Take it up to Amsterdam and 98th, okay?"

"Sure. No problem." He looked at the guy through the rear-view, the guy still breathing hard and sweating. Glancing back out the window, still worried about shirtsleeves. Like his ladyfriend's irate hubby had found some other cab and was hot on his tail. It only happened in the movies.

"So what's the story, you don't mind my asking? You mean you didn't know?"

"Hell, no, I didn't know. It was a pickup in a bar. She's got her hand on my leg for godsakes. It's going great. Then this guy shows up. Says he's gonna push my face in! Jesus, I never even paid the bar-tab! I just got the hell out of there. Thank god for *you*, man!"

Lenny reflected that nobody had ever thanked god for him before. Not that he could remember. It was a first.

Your Good Deed for the Day, he thought. From the look of the shirtsleeves, maybe for the month.

"So you go back, you pay your tab another time. No problem."

"I don't even know the name of the place. I just wandered in."

"Corner of 58th and 10th? That would be the Landmark Grill."

The guy nodded. He saw it in the rearview mirror.

And there was something in the guy's face right then he didn't like. Something nasty all of a sudden. Like the guy had gone away somewhere and left a different guy sitting in the back seat who only looked like him.

Ah, the guy's had a hard night, he thought.

No babe. No pickup. Almost got his ass kicked for his trouble. You might be feeling nasty too.

They drove in silence after that until Lenny dropped him at Amsterdam and 98th, northeast corner. The guy said thanks and left him exactly fifteen per cent over the meter. Not bad but not exactly great either, considering. The next fare took him to the East Side and the next four down to the Village and then Soho and Alphabet City and then to the Village again. He never did get back to Tenth or even to Hell's Kitchen for that matter.

So it was only when he returned to the lot at the end of his shift that he learned from his dispatcher that the Landmark Grill had been robbed at gunpoint by a tallish thin sandy-haired man in a parka. Who got away in a cab, for chrissake. Everybody was buzzing about it because he'd used a goddamn cab as getaway. Thought it was pretty funny.

That and the fact that the bartender had been crazy enough to chase him.

A guy with a gun. You had to be nuts to risk it.

Or maybe you had to be bleeding from the head where the guy had used the butt end of his gun on you. Lenny hadn't managed to catch that little detail in the rear-view.

There was never any question in his mind about calling the cops. If they didn't have his medallion number then so be it. You didn't want to get involved in something like this unless you had to. But Lenny thought about his fifteen per cent over the meter and wondered what the take was like.

No good deed ever goes unpunished his mother used to say.

He hated to admit it but as in most things, he supposed his mom was right.

TWO

At first Elise was embarrassed by them. No—*for* them.

First embarrassed. Then fascinated.

And then she couldn't look away.

The train was real late—she'd wondered if it was another bomb scare somewhere up the line, it would be just her luck to miss her dance class entirely and it was the only class she could care about at all—so that the platform was crowded and getting more so, mostly kids like her just out of school for the day and *thank god it was over*, nobody but Elise seeming to care if the train was late or not, the noise level enormous with the echo of kids shouting, laughing, arguing, whatever.

For sure these two over by the pillar there didn't care. She doubted they even noticed the kids swarming around them. Much less the lateness of the train.

She had never seen a pair of adults so...*into* one another.

But it wasn't a good thing.

It was terrible. And it was going on and on.

They were probably in their thirties, forties—Elise couldn't tell but she thought they were younger than her mother—and the woman was a little taller than the man who was almost as cute, for an old guy, as she was pretty. Or they would have been cute and pretty if their faces didn't keep...*crumbling* all the time.

They kept hugging and pulling apart and staring at each other as though trying to memorize one another's faces and then hugging again so hard she thought it must have hurt sometimes, she could see the man's fingers digging deep into the back of her blouse. And both of them were crying, tears just pouring down their cheeks and they didn't even bother to try to wipe them away half the time, they mostly just let them come.

She saw them stop and smile at each other and the smiles were worse than the tears. *My god, they're so sad.* And smiling seemed to bring the tears on again, like they were one and the same, coming from the very same place. It was like they couldn't stop. Like she was watching two hearts breaking for ever and ever.

She was already ten or fifteen feet away from them but she found herself stepping back without even knowing at first she was doing it. It was as though there were some kind of magnetic field around them that repelled instead of pulling, as though they were pushing out at empty space, in order to give them space, all the space they needed to perform this horrible dance.

I meant what I said, you know that, right? she heard the woman tell him and he nodded and took her in his arms again and she missed what the woman said after that but then they were crying again though real silently this time and then she heard the woman say say I *just can't anymore* and then they were crying hard again, really sobbing, clutching each other and their shoulders shaking and she wanted to look away because what if they noticed her staring at them but somehow she knew that they weren't going to notice, they weren't going to notice anything but each other.

They were splitting up, she knew now. At first she'd thought maybe they had a kid who'd died or something. I *just can't anymore.* The woman was dumping him but she didn't want to because they still loved each other. And they loved each other *so much*—she'd never seen two people that much in love. She wasn't even sure she'd ever seen it in the movies.

So how could you do that? How could you just break up if you felt that way? How was it even possible?

She noticed that some of the other kids were watching too and would go silent for a while. Not as intently as Elise was watching and mostly the girls but there on the platform you could feel it pouring out of these people and it was getting to some of the other kids as well. Something was happening to them that she had the feeling only adults knew about, something secret played out right out there in the open. Something she sensed was important. And a little scary.

If this was what being an adult was all about she wanted no part of it.

And yet she did.

To be in love that much? God! So much in love that nothing and nobody matters but the two of you standing together right where you're standing, oblivious to everybody, just holding tight and feeling something, *somebody,* so much and deep. It must be wonderful.

It must be awful.

It must be both together.

How? How could that be?

So that as the train roared in and kids crowded into the car, Elise behind them, wiping at her own tears which only served to confuse her more now, the woman stepped on a little behind her to the side and turned to the window, hands pressed to the dirty cloudy glass to watch him standing there alone on the platform and somehow smaller-looking without her and Elise looked from one to the other and back again and saw their shattered smiles.

THREE

She put down the paper and washed her hands in the sink. As usual the Sunday *Times* was filthy with printer's ink. She went back to her easel in the living room. Her lunch-break was over. The pastel was coming along.

She had that much, anyway. The work.

What did you expect? she thought. When things got bad they were probably bound to get worse. If only for a little while.

She hoped it was only for a little while.

Because she was seriously doubting, for the very first time ever, her actual survival here.

Everybody in the city was fragile, she guessed. No matter where you were or who you were World Trade had touched you somehow. Even if you'd lost nobody close to you, you'd still lost something. She knew that was part of it.

She could look at a cat in a window and start to cry.

And breaking off with David would have been bad enough under any circumstances—correction, still was bad enough. Because he wouldn't quite let go and neither could she exactly. Lonely late-night e-mails still were all too common between them.

> *I understand you can't see me, I understand it hurts too much to keep seeing me and I'm sorry. But I miss just talking to you too. We always talked, even through the worst of it. E-mails just don't work. I feel like I've lost not only my lover but my friend. Please— call me sometime, okay? I want my friend back. I want her bad.*
> *Love, David.*

> *I can't call. Not yet. Someday maybe but not now. I'd call and we'd talk and the next step would be seeing you and you know that. Why do you want to make me go through this again, David? Jesus! You say you understand but you don't seem to. You're not going to leave her and that's that. And I need somebody who'll be there for me all the time, not just a couple nights a week. I miss you too but you're not that person, David. You can't be. And I can't simply wish that away. So please, for a while, just please leave me be.*
> *Love, Claire.*

She knew he was hurting and she hated that because there was so much good between them and the love was still there. She hated hurting him. But she was alone and he wasn't. So she also knew who was hurting the worst. She was. She was tired of crying herself to sleep every night he wouldn't be there next to her or every morning when he'd leave. It had to stop.

He'd never stop it. It was up to her.

She'd been alone most of her life but that was always basically okay. She liked her own company. She'd always been a loner.

But she'd never felt this lonely.

What was that Bob Dylan line? *I'm sick of love.*

She knew exactly how he felt when he wrote it.

Fuck it, she thought, *get to work. You're an artist. So make art.*

The piece was one of a series, a still-life, an apple core surrounded by chains. A padlock lay open, gleaming, embracing one of the links of chain.

She studied it.

She knew exactly what it meant. Most people didn't. That was fine, so long as they *felt* it.

And bought one now and then.

Which hadn't happened in a while now.

Concentrate, she thought. Focus. Work the blacks. Work the shadows.

But that was the other thing. Money. Cold hard cash. Financially her life was a mess too. She'd only just started painting again—David was the main one who'd encouraged her, dammit!—had only sold a few pieces for good but not terrific money, and the New York restaurant business, which she'd always counted on as backup, had been hit hard by the Bush economy even before World Trade Center. Tourism was down to a fraction of what it was this time last year and the natives were paranoid about going out to dinner. In the past three months she'd been laid off as a bartender, hired as a waitress, laid off as a waitress, hired as a manager—a job she'd always loathed—and then laid off as a manager too.

She was always assured it was a matter of cutbacks, not her performance. Last hired, first fired. Simple as that.

She'd been making the rounds. Nobody was hiring.

So that at the moment she was jobless, with two months' rent and utilities in the bank and if she didn't find something soon she was going to have to eat this apple core off the canvas.

It's Sunday, she thought. You can't do a damn thing about it now.

So make the art. Later, call your mother.

Get on with it. All of it.

She drew a line, smudged it lightly with her finger. A link of chain sprung suddenly into focus on the canvas. She drew another.

FOUR

What the hell are you doing? He thought.

It was two in the morning. He was standing outside across the street from her apartment. He could see the light burning through the second-floor living room window. Either she was still awake or she'd fallen asleep and left it on but to leave it on was very unlike her.

She was awake.

He could walk up the steps, ring the bell.

No he couldn't.

He had no right to. It would be tantamount to harassment.

And standing out here was tantamount to stalking.

So what the hell are you doing, David?

A glimpse, he thought. That's all. A glimpse of somebody you love through a brownstone window. What the hell is wrong with that?

Everything. It's crazy, desperate. It's pathetic. You're not Romeo and she's not Juliet. Go the hell home.

Don't want to.

Your wife is waiting.

By now she'll be fast asleep.

You've had too much to drink again.

So? What else is new?

Go home.

A cab cruised past him going west. Northwest was the direction of his apartment. The cab's sign was lit. He could have flagged it down. A simple wave of the hand. He didn't. He needed something. He wanted to *feel something.*

Now what the hell does that *mean?*

59th was quiet. No breeze. Nobody on the street but him. There was traffic heading south on 9th half a block away but not here and even on 9th the traffic was light, he could barely hear it hissing by.

So here he was, alone. Staring up at a living-room window and afraid to look away or even to blink for fear that if he did it would be exactly that moment she'd choose to appear and not any other moment and not again, afraid of the perversity of incident and chance, perhaps because it was precisely incident and chance that had got him here in the first place. She a new bartender, he a regular. Quickly becoming friends, far more slowly becoming lovers—two years before that happened—not until a casual date that left them alone in a crowded noisy new dance club they found not to their liking at all, waiting for two other friends to return from the bar so they could get the hell out of there, a single slightly boozy hug turning to a surprisingly lovely kiss and then more and more and before they knew it two more years had gone by and love had trapped them as surely incident and chance could trap anyone.

The window blurred over.

He wiped his eyes.

He was aware of sirens in the distance, somewhere around Times Square.

The window blurred again.

Were the sirens doing this? Some fucking *ambulance* making him cry? Somebody else's distress? Some stranger's? It was possible. These days anything was.

But that was too damn ridiculous even for him and no, he saw what it was now, literally saw it in that way that the mind imposes an image it chooses over the eyes so that what the eyes see in the natural world disappears for a moment, unable to compete, utterly sterile compared to the image the brain mandates. He saw it, vividly, sobbed once because he knew that in the natural world he might never see it again and certainly not the way he did now, directed so wholly at him—her open happy smile—and turned and started home.

FIVE

The composite on the nightly news was not great.

They'd got the nose right and the chin mostly but the forehead was way too high and the eyes were completely wrong because the eyes in the composite were bland, they held nothing, while his were full of...

...what?

Something. He didn't bother trying to go there.

They were off on the numbers too. They had him down for

around fifteen, twenty jobs this year. He had to laugh. The number was more like thirty, thirty-five. Roughly one every week and a half. He figured that by the end of his own personal fiscal year which began and ended on his birthday just before Christmas he'd take in fifty, maybe sixty grand. Not as much as if you were robbing banks but bars were a whole lot safer. Bars were vulnerable.

For one thing you didn't work in daylight except to cruise for likely joints to hit. You didn't have much in the way of surveillance cameras to worry about. And you didn't have some retired cop with an attitude, some asshole armed guard willing and stupid enough to start blazing away at you.

It was a pretty rare bartender who was willing to die for the till and his tips.

That guy last week, though. That asshole actually *chasing* him.

He thought he'd put the fear of god in him. Especially that last hard whack on the head. He guessed there had to be a first time for everything.

Usually the getaway was simple. You headed for the nearest subway, didn't matter where you went once you were on it. If there was a bus handy you caught that. You got off and had a beer or two at another bar far away and then you went on home.

They'd worried out loud on the news about his gun. Some police lieutenant mouthing off. Said that seeing as he *had* a gun, sooner or later he was going to use it. That was bullshit. His weapons were surprise and fear. The gun was only window-dressing. Loaded window-dressing but window-dressing all the same.

Then they tried to link him up to a wider trend. All very ominous. Seems that shootings in the City were up twenty-four percent over the same month last year—the figure spiked by the thinned ranks of the NYPD who were now on anthrax, security and ground zero duty since World Trade Center instead of manning street crime.

Again, bullshit. He wasn't part of any goddamn trend. He just did what he always did.

Plain old-fashioned armed robbery.

He sat on the sofa and sipped his beer. The composite didn't worry him. Except for the eyes he was blessed with one of those more or less *basic* faces, a kind of no-frills face, one that set off no bells and whistles in anybody. *Acceptable*—that was how he liked to think about it. Acceptable enough so that guys had no reason either to fear him, be impressed or intimidated by him or even to remember him for that matter. Acceptable enough to women so that he got himself some pussy now and then. Not a hard face and not soft. No scars, no dimples, no cleft palates or cleft chins.

The composite didn't work. His face was far too mutable.

The hair you could cut or color. For the line of forehead, a hat or a baseball cap. You could change the eyes with colored contact lenses or no-scrip glasses or just by trimming down your eyebrows a bit. Or darkening them with eyebrow pencil.

He thought eyebrows were seriously underrated.

You wanted to avoid a good tan. A good tan was memorable to New Yorkers, who were used to pallor. You made the mistake getting of a tan, you powdered it. Physique was changeable as the goddamn weather. You're on the tall side like he was? five-eleven? So you're stoop-shouldered now and then. You flex the knees. Build? Baggy sweaters or business clothes one time, jeans and tee-shirt the next.

Backpack on one job, shopping bag or briefcase on another.

He finished the beer and frowned at New York One. New York One was supposed to be about New York City, wasn't it? But now they were going on and on about the fucking anthrax again. If it wasn't the anthrax it was the fucking war in Afghanistan or else the fucking World Trade Center. Who cared if some senator's assistant or postal clerk got anthrax—inhaled, cutaneous, or shot up the ass? Who cared if the towelheads took out skyscrapers?

He strictly worked ground-floor.

They ended with some puff piece about this guy who had to be the most politically correct asshole on the face of the earth—some Westchester dentist who was offering to buy up all the neighborhood kids' Halloween candy so they didn't rot their teeth. Fuck their teeth. He turned the damn thing off and got up and tossed the beercan into the sink.

Time to get.

In the bathroom shaving he glanced down at his various toiletry items and got a really great idea.

"You're lucky," the bartender said. "I was just about to tell my friend here last call. What'll it be?"

"Miller, thanks."

"Miller coming up."

The barkeep's *friend* probably didn't know him from Adam. His *friend* looked to have been on a long night's pub crawl and only one step up from blue-collar, if that, while this was clearly a kids' bar, Barrow and Hudson, pool table and concert posters, "Sweet Home Alabama" on the jukebox and the bartender not much more than a kid himself. Wire-rim glasses, rosy cheeks, spiked hair, good strong build under the tee-shirt. Irish maybe.

"Gettin' cold out there?"

The kid poured a half glass of Miller into the beer mug and set it down in front of him.

"Nah. Good breeze, though."

The barkeep took his twenty to the register. The guy next to him downed his beer and mumbled thanks and slid off the barstool and tapped his dollar fifty with his forefinger. He was tipping the bartender one fifty. Big spender. He put his hands in his pockets and headed for the door. Which meant that this was going very nicely indeed.

"G'night. Thank you, sir. You take care now."

The barkeep put his change in front of him. Scooped up his tip and dropped it in the bucket.

He slipped on the surgical gloves.

"*You* take care," he said.

"S'cuse me?"

They said that a lot. *You take care.* You said it back to them, it threw them off balance. Maybe even started to worry them right then and there.

But this kid was only puzzled.

He slid the .45 out from behind his sport jacket. Rested it flat on the bar pointed at the barkeep's trim flat belly.

"I said *you* take care. Now, listen real carefully and you'll get to go home tonight to your girlfriend. Let's say I'm an old college buddy of yours and I'm closing up with you, so you do what you do every night, only I'm here. That's how I want you to act. I'm just here having a drink. You lock the door and hit the lights outside and you dim the ones in here. Only difference is after that you go to the register and instead of counting it you empty it into this bag."

He handed the Big Brown Bag from Bloomie's across the counter.

"Open it and put it on the floor. That's it. Very good. Now go about your business. And don't even think about opening that door. I know you really want to but see, it takes too long to open it, throw it back and then go through. You'll be dead by the time you hit the sidewalk, believe me. They've already got me down twice for Murder One"—*it was a lie but it always worked*—"so it doesn't mean a thing to me one way or the other. I'm a very good shot, though. So it would mean a lot to you."

For emphasis he clicked off the safety.

He could smell it then, that faint ammonia smell or something like ammonia. Bleach maybe. Fear-sweat coming off the guy. Fear cleansing the guy, pouring through the fat and skin all the way up from the organs, the organs unwilling to cease their function, unwilling to give up the pulse.

He put the gun between his legs and swiveled on the stool smiling as the guy moved on shaky legs out from behind the bar and fished his keys out of his pocket, locked the door, put them back in his pocket and reached behind a tall brown sad potted cactus and flicked off the outside lights.

"The dimmer's over here, okay?"

The guy was pointing across the room to another half-dead fern or something.

"Why shouldn't it be okay? I trust you. What's your name?"

The guy hesitated. Like he didn't want to say. Like it was getting personal.

"Robert...Bob."

"Bob or Robert?"

"Bob."

"Okay, Bob. Let's dim the lights."

He watched him cross the room, not even daring to glance out through the plate-glass window, afraid that even that much might get him shot. Good.

It was always amazing to him. Within minutes—seconds—you could get a guy performing for you like a trained seal. Half the time, like now, you didn't even have to ask.

"You should water your fucking plants, Bob. Know that?"

He nodded, reached up and dimmed the lights. "Okay, Bob, let's get to the good stuff."

He drank some of his beer. The barkeep moved back behind the bar and keyed open the register.

"Just the bills, now. No change."

He watched him drop the bills into the Bloomies bag. Bob had had a pretty good night tonight. From where he sat it looked like well over a thousand. He'd read in the paper today that business was down in the City about $357 million since September 11th. Bars and restaurants particularly. You wouldn't know it from where he was sitting.

"Tell you what, Bob. Let's play a little game for your tip bucket. I'm sure you got a couple hundred in there. I'm sure you'd like to keep it. So. I lose, it's yours. I win, it goes in the bag."

"No, that's okay, you can just..."

He started reaching for the bucket above the register.

"Hey! It's *not* okay, Bob!"

He lurched to his feet and leaned over and shoved the barrel of the gun against the barkeep's pale high forehead. He could feel the guy trembling right down though to the handle of the gun. Saw his glasses slip half an inch down his sweaty nose.

"Get this right, Robert. I say we play a little game, then we play a little game. Let me tell you something you don't know about me, Bob. I don't like people. In fact it's fair to say that I fucking hate people. Not just you, *Bob*, you spikey-haired little Midwest shit-for-brains—though I do hate you, for sure. But see, I hate *everybody*. I'm a completely equal-opportunity hater—Jews, Arabs, Asians, blacks, WASPS, you name it. Some people think that's a problem. You know how many people have tried to help me with this little problem, Bob? Have tried to *reform* me? Dozens! I'm not kidding you. But you know, it never takes. Never. You know why? Because my one real kick in life, the one thing that really gets me off, is to reform all those people who want to reform me. And it is my honestly held belief that the only way to reform people is to hurt 'em or kill 'em or both. Period."

He sat back down again, rested the gun on the bar, his hand spread out on top of it.

Bob was visibly twitching now, mouth gulping air like a fish.

"Jesus, calm down, Robert, or this isn't gonna work. Hand me the bag. And your keys. That's good. Thanks very much. Now slide over that cutting board there and that little knife you use on the lemons."

"Oh, jesus."

"Just do it. And dump the lemons."

The kid glanced at his hand on the gun and then turned and did as he was told, set the knife and the board down in front of him.

"Okay, here's what we're gonna do. You're right-handed, right? Thought so. So you're gonna put your right hand down, *palm-side up*—that's important, palm up—and spread your fingers. Then I'm gonna take this knife here, which I notice you keep nice and sharp—very good Robert—and jab around between your fingers. Slow at first, then maybe a little faster. Not too fast, don't worry. Believe me, I'm good at this. I really am. But if I miss, even the slightest little cut, the slightest nick, you get to keep the bucket. I don't miss, bucket goes with me. Fair enough? Sure it is. All you got to do is hold very still for me now."

"Oh jesus."

"Stop with the *oh jesus*, Robert. Try to be a fucking man for a change. Or you can just remember that I got the gun here, whichever works for you. Okay. Spread your fingers."

The kid pushed his glasses up on his nose. They slid back down again. Then he took a deep breath and held it and put his hand down flat on the board.

He took the knife between his thumb on one side and forefinger and middle finger on the other and as promised, he started off slow. *Thump*, beat. *Thump*, beat. *Thump*. Then he picked up tempo and the thumps got louder because the force got greater and he really was good at this, damn he was good, *thumpthumpthumpthumpthumpthumpthump* and the kid kept saying *oh jesus, oh jesus*, Bob a Christian through and through now and he knew that for poor Bob this was going on forever, this was an eternity and when he finally got tired out scaring the shit out of the kid pinned the web of his thumb to the cutting board so that the kid gasped and said *aahhhh!* and he said *don't you yell, Bob, whatever you do, don't you dare fucking yell.*

And Bob didn't. Bob was toughing it out as expected.

He just stood there breathing hard, his left elbow propping him up on the bar against the pain and probably against a pair of pretty shaky legs and looked down at the spreading pool of blood between his fingers. He reached into his pocket and took out the envelope and opened it. Tore it down one side and blew a tablespoon of Johnson's talcum powder directly into his face.

Bob looked startled. Blinking at him, confused.

"*Anthrax, Bob,*" he said. "It's the real thing, I promise."

He picked up the bag of money. Took four pair of rolled-up socks out of his jacket pockets and unrolled them and spread them out over the money.

Like he'd just done his laundry.

"You try not to breathe now for a while Bob, go wash your face. That shit'll get right down into your lungs. And you know what happens then. Bucket's yours. You won it fair and square. You take care now. And if you think I've treated you badly which I really hope you don't, well hell, you should just see what I do to the ladies."

Whether the kid believed him or not about the anthrax didn't matter but he was betting he'd have a bad moment at least, the City being what it was nowadays.

He keyed the lock, looked right and left, threw the keys in the gutter and slipped off the gloves as he walked on out the door.

SIX

It had taken Claire a while to do this, to work up the will and the courage finally and Barbara had felt the same way. So they'd decided to do it together and that helped.

They stood in front of the Chambers Street subway exit on an unseasonably warm sunny day along with thirty or so other people scattered across the block staring south from behind the police barricades at the distant sliver of sky where only a month and a half ago the Twin Towers had been.

The smell was invasive, raw, born on a northerly breeze. It clawed at her throat. *Superheated metal, melting plastic and something else. Something she didn't like to think about.*

She had never much liked the Trade Center. It had always seemed overbearing, soulless, a huge smug temple to money and power.

And now both she and Barbara were quietly crying.

All those people lost.

She was crying so much these days.

She knew nobody who had died here.

Somehow she seemed to know everybody who had died here.

She stared up into a bright blue sky tarnished with plumes of pale blonde smoke and after a while she turned around.

She had never seen so many stricken faces.

Old people and young people and even little kids—kids so small she thought they shouldn't even know about this let alone be standing here, they shouldn't have to grow up in the wake of it either. It wasn't right. A woman wearing jeans and an I LOVE NY— EVEN MORE tee-shirt was wiping back a steady stream of tears. A man with a briefcase didn't bother.

She didn't see a single smile.

"Let's walk," she said.

It was a whisper, really. As though they were standing in a church. And that was the other uncanny thing about this—the silence. New York City heavy and thick with silence broken only by the occasional truck rolling by filled with debris and once, the wail of a fire engine hurtling through the streets to ground zero. She had only one memory of the City to compare it with—a midnight stroll a few years back after a record snowfall, a snowfall big enough so that it had closed all the airports and bridges and tunnels. It had paralyzed the City. She remembered standing alone in the middle of the northbound lane at Broadway and 68th Street in pristine untracked snow for over twenty minutes until finally a pair of headlights appeared far in the distance. She could have been in Vermont or New Hampshire. Instead she was standing in one of the busiest streets in the busiest city in the world. She remembered being delighted with the sheer novelty of it, of all that peace and silence.

This was not the same thing.

They walked south down Broadway past shop after shop selling posters or framed photos of the Towers, their eyes inevitably drawn to them. And they didn't strike her as crass or even commercial particularly, though of course they were—New York would always recover first through commerce—they stuck her as valid reminders of what had been. And there was nothing wrong with that.

They stopped in front of a boarded-up Chase Bank filthy with dust, the entire broad surface of its window covered with ID photos of cops and firemen dead, all those young faces staring out at them frozen in time forever. The thick brown-white dust lay everywhere. On the sidewalks, the streets, the surfaces of shops and highrises— canopies and even whole skyscrapers were being hosed down to try to get rid of it.

It was a losing battle. The site was still burning.

She stared at the faces moving past her. She guessed that not one in thirty was smiling.

They passed police barricades strewn with flowers.

Windows filled with appeals for information on the missing. *The dead.*

Their photos.

They passed children's bright crayon drawings—hearts, firemen, cops, flowers, words of grief and thanks.

It had been a while since either of them had said a thing. She'd always been perfectly comfortable with Barbara ever since their days bartending together at the Village Café but this was different. Each of them, she thought, was really alone here. Everybody was.

The wind shifted. The stench died down. But her mouth still tasted like steel and dust and plastic. She was hungry. She hadn't eaten. Yet it was impossible to think of eating here. She wondered how the sub shops and sidewalk stands stayed open. Even a Coke or a bottled water here would taste...wrong.

They'd stop at each corner and gaze into the empty sky.

Approaching Liberty Street the sidewalks became more crowded and then very crowded and before long they were trapped in the midst of a slow-moving mass of people that was almost frightening, what felt like hundreds of people, tourists and New Yorkers all crowding together at the barricades and straining for what was supposedly the best view of what was no longer there. And here you did see smiles and laughter, too damn much laughter for her liking. Almost a carnival atmosphere, fueled by morbid curiosity. And packed too tight together, far too tight, seven or eight deep—so that what if something happened? what if somebody panicked? You could be crushed, trampled. And when a father snapped a photo of his smiling little girl against the horizon and then a teenage boy with his girlfriend did the same she said, *let's get the hell out of here.*

"We can't," said Barbara.

"I don't like this."

"Neither do I."

She was shaking with a mix of fear and fury.

"This way."

It was easier than she'd thought. As they stepped slowly through from the center to the rear of the crowd people were happy to take their place so they could get nearer to the site. Finally they stood at the edge of this crawling human tide, their backs nearly scraping the filthy storefronts and climbing over steps leading into other storefronts and soon they found themselves on Park Row leading east so that it was silent again finally and they laughed and shook their heads almost dizzy with relief and that was when they heard it, a small soft mewling sound.

"Is that...?"

"Shhhh," she said. "Yes."

She listened. In a moment she heard it again. There was a long green dumpster on blocks and packed with rubble, mostly chunks of cement, across the street to her left. The sound was coming from there. They walked over and peered beneath the dumpster, Claire working one way, Barbara the other.

"Nothing," she said.

"Nothing here either."

She looked behind it. A dirty empty sidewalk and the wall of a building.

"We didn't imagine that," Barbara said. "That was a kitten."

"I know. Hold on a minute."

She put her foot down on one of the blocks and hauled herself up to the lip of the dumpster and scanned the rubble.

And there it was, far over to her right, a tiny tabby walking unsteadily across a narrow jagged cement-shard tightrope, back and forth, gazing down at something beyond her sight-lines to the far side of the dumpster. They heard it cry again. She hopped down.

"Over here," she said.

They walked over to where she judged the cat had been but there weren't any blocks there, nothing for her to step up on. She looked around for a milk crate or a bucket or garbage can. Something.

"Cradle your fingers."

"Gotcha."

Barbara did and her first try failed miserably and Claire fell back to the street again practically into her and they both started laughing and then she tried again.

"Okay. I got it. Hold on."

She took most of her weight out of Barbara's hands when her belly hit the lip of the dumpster and she folded at the waist and she spotted the cat and reached and the kitten turned to look at her, wide-eyed at this new disturbance and she thought it probably would have bolted had it not been perched there so precariously, but as it was, stayed put just long enough for her to put her right hand down and push further at the lip to get an extra foot of reach so that she caught it in her left hand and lifted it away.

The kitten gave one long *meeeeeooooowwwww* in earnest now and glanced anxiously over its shoulder and she looked down to where the cat was looking and saw the much larger body whose markings so nearly matched its own. Its head lay hidden beneath a block of stone. She saw long-dried blood along its bib and shoulder.

"Oh, you poor little thing," she said.

The kitten just looked at her, trembling.

"I've got her," she said. "I'm coming down."

"How did you know?" Barbara said.

"How did I know what?"

"That it was a she?"

She laughed. "I did. I didn't. I don't know."

They were headed uptown and over to the subway and then home. Barbara carried her bag for her. She carried the kitten pressed against her breast and shoulder. The kitten was matted and caked with dust and god knows what else and smelled like the inside of a garbage can and she gripped Claire's shoulder fiercely. Claire didn't mind a bit.

"How old, do you figure? Five, six weeks?"

"God, I doubt that her eyes were even open a week ago. She's young. Really young. I'll get her to a vet this afternoon. Check her out and see if she's okay. The vet'll probably know."

They were going back roughly the way they came. Past the

dusty shops and into the smell of burning and the strange sad New York silence.

"You going to keep her?"

She lifted the cat off her body and held her up over her head with both hands and the cat looked down and she smiled at the cat and smiled too out into the quiet street.

"Forever."

NOVEMBER 10TH, 2001

SEVEN

When David finished work for the day—the acrylic for the YA book cover was getting somewhere, finally—he did what he always did and cleaned his brushes and covered his canvas and went to the bedroom and pressed MESSAGES on his answering machine and turned off the mute button and listened.

Sandwiched between a recorded pitch from Mike Bloomberg asking for his support in the coming election and a call from his agent's assistant asking him to phone when he got the chance, she had good news for him, was her voice saying *it's me, just wanted to see how you were doing,* cut off abruptly.

There had been whole days by now that he hadn't even thought of her though they were still few and far between but this had been one of them, he'd been that absorbed in the work for a change, and then her voice, or the ghost of her voice—his machine was an old analog cassette recorder and had the annoying habit of allowing snippets of old buried messages to rise up from between the new ones like withered fingers from a grave—rushed at him with all its force and broke the dam inside him again.

How am I doing?

Some days fine, Claire. Most days, not well at all.

He dialed her number. Something he hadn't done in weeks now at her request.

He got her machine.

"It's me," he said. "Did you phone today? Or is my machine messing with my mind again? I figured I'd better check. Anyway, I'm here, and I hope all's well. See you."

He'd given her plenty of time to pick up. She hadn't, so either she really wasn't there and the call had come in earlier or her voice had been a mechanical glitch and she still wasn't talking to him.

Ready to talk to him was the way she put it.

He'd wondered if she'd ever be ready.

His agent was on speed-dial. She wasn't. He'd taken her off almost a month ago. *Too much temptation, far too easy.* His agent said they had a terrific offer for him, cover art for the next six Anne Rice paperback reissues, his agent very enthusiastic about it, and went on to outline the deal. The deal was a good one and he sure as hell could use the money but he'd worked with Rice a few years back and knew she could be a pain in the ass, one of those writers who seemed to think they were painters too and let you know it each step of the way, detailing you to death, your art going back and forth for approval like a canvas ping-pong ball.

"Tell them I'll take it," he said.

He hung up and went to his computer and lit his twenty-first cigarette of the day. It was supposed to help him cut down if he counted them but so far it had only made him nervous to know he was smoking so damn much. He went into his e-mail. Half an hour later he hadn't answered any of them. The words wouldn't come.

It was obsessive but all he could think of was her message on the machine. *Just wanted to see how you were doing.* Maybe she really did. Maybe she had just gone out for a while and she'd call back later.

He doubted it.

But he missed her enormously and whenever he allowed himself to realize that, whenever he truly let it through, he'd cling to even the most delicate thread of hope. *She'd changed her mind, it didn't matter that he couldn't bring himself to leave, she missed him too much, all forgiven, let's try again.*

He knew her far too well to think it was anything but fantasy but he clung to hope as though hope itself might make it so. It wasn't just the sex he missed though god knows it had never been anything but fine between them but his heart had an entire Whole Earth catalog of what he missed about her and his mind kept flipping through the pages. Sometimes almost at random, something striking him hard for no reason. *The gap between her two front teeth, the husky voice, the talk about mutual friends whose names he hadn't heard for weeks now and incidents long past and people long gone in both their lives and art and books and feelings, the tall proud way she walked the street or the feel of her waist beneath his arm or her cheek beneath his hand or the two of them staring up at the darkening New York sky—it* just went on and on. Countless images, moments observed and shared over the heady course of two long years. And the friendship which always lay beneath.

He pushed back away from the computer and turned it off, watched the screen crackle down to neutral gray. The email would have to wait. He wasn't feeling up to the basically cheery voice it always seemed to require of him

A drink, he thought, *that's what was in order. You got a lot of work done today. You deserve it. Have a scotch and turn on the news for a while. Couldn't hurt.*

Could it?

He was drinking a fair amount these days.

Was it for pleasure the way it used to be? Or just to throw a cozy blanket over pain?

He knew Sara worried about it. Sometimes so did he.

He seemed to have to bludgeon himself to sleep these days.

He got up and poured one anyway. His two tabby cats yawned awake on the counter when he cracked the plastic tray of ice. He scratched them both behind the ears. They fell asleep again. Sara wouldn't be home from work for two hours yet and the cats wouldn't be fed until she did. They knew that as well as they knew every flat surface in the apartment and the exact extent to which it was good for sleeping on. Until that time rolled around, dozing was an appropriate response to life.

He wished he were as sensible and poured himself a stiff one.

He was waiting for a phone call.

It might be a long night.

It was.

Seven hours, five drinks and a leftover chicken dinner later she hadn't called. So it had been a glitch, as suspected. Tomorrow he was getting a new machine, dammit. He didn't need the torment.

And it *was* a torment. He wasn't overstating. He felt like a caged animal in his own apartment. Sara was in the bedroom watching TV and doing paperwork, some homework from the bank but he couldn't join her the way he usually did, not tonight. He couldn't turn it off. It was as though being in the same room with her right now would constitute betrayal—of Sara, of Claire, of all three of them.

He tried to read but that didn't work either. He never painted or even sketched when he'd been drinking and he wasn't about to start now. So that left the computer. He answered his e-mail as best he could and then surfed the net, looking for images, not sure what he was looking for but something to startle him or comfort him. Something. He felt hot-wired to her voice on the phone. Finally he left-clicked on the WRITE MAIL icon and began this long, feverish, idiotic letter to her. A plea for some kind of communication, any kind would do but mostly he wanted to see her and probably he wanted that for the very same reason she did not want to see him. It might start it up all over again, which he was selfish enough to want even knowing it could not be good for her was and honest enough about to make him feel guilty as sin.

He didn't know if the booze was helping or hindering in the sense-making department but the letter poured out of him and when it was finished he began to hit the SEND button but then stopped to read it again. He didn't know if it spoke to his feelings or didn't. If it was self-pitying drivel or not. *Fuck it,* he thought. *Fuck it fuck it fuck it.* He saved it into the MAIL WAITING TO BE SENT file. Maybe he'd send it off tomorrow when he was more sober and maybe he wouldn't.

Meantime he was not going to sit here staring at a computer screen all night.

He knew where she worked these days.

They still had a few friends in common who hadn't deserted him completely and he'd persuaded Barbara to give up the address. Hell, she was right here in the neighborhood. Only ten blocks away.

He turned off the computer and got up and walked into the bedroom. Sara looked up at him from the bed. Piles of papers fanned out in front of her in an orderly fashion. She was doing something to them with a red felt tip pen.

"I'm going out," he said. "Feeling restless."

"Okay. Where to?"

"Take a walk, have a drink. We'll see."

"You going to see Claire?"

"I don't know. Maybe. I guess I'll figure that one out once I'm out there. She still doesn't want to see me."

She put down the pen.

"David, are we in trouble? Do we need to talk?"

"No, we're not in trouble. At least not now. I don't know about the long run. I don't know where we're going. But we don't need to talk, not now."

"I worry."

"Don't. It's okay. I just might need to see her. I don't know."

She looked at him and nodded. "All right. Be careful," she said. She meant it. All that *careful* entailed.

"I will. I love you."

She went back to her papers. He thought how strange this would look to some outsider. As though she really didn't care. But he knew she did care and how much. They had thirty years together and the ties were strong even if sometimes invisible to most people, stretched thin these days because he had fallen in love and she of course knew as she knew everything important in his life—and maybe it was that knowing, as much as the cats they shared or the apartment they shared or the fact that she was his first best critic or even the years themselves of order and easy companionship which was why he stayed and couldn't seem to leave.

Sarah was family by now. He had no other.

He put on his jacket and stepped into the hall and locked the door behind him.

EIGHT

Half-past midnight and Claire was *finally* getting to eat—the Caesar salad with grilled chicken she'd asked the cook to leave for her in the microwave. They'd been slammed all night long for a change but now there was only old Willie in his usual corner, arms folded in front of him and half asleep over his beer. When she finished she'd roust him. Willie weighed in at a good two hundred pounds and he'd already fallen off his barstool once since she'd started working here only a few weeks ago. He was going to crack his head open one of these days. She didn't want it to be on her watch.

Sandi dumped the last of the candles out of its holder into the black plastic trash bag down at the end of the bar, sighed and smiled and untied her waitress' apron and slid it off over her head.

"I'm outa here, that okay?"

They'd already split the tips and balanced out the register. There hadn't been any discrepancies between that and the cash-due printout or they'd have had to go through the checks together one by one to find the error. And Sandi looked dead on her feet.

"Sure. Go. You have a good night."

"What's left of it."

"Give that guy a hug for me."

"Yeah. Hey, listen, I really want to thank you for that. I really appreciate you talking to me. It helped."

"Kenny's a good kid. Everybody screws up now and then. Just don't let him make a habit of it, that's all."

Sandi smiled again and slipped on her jacket and hoisted her shoulderbag.

"I won't. See you tomorrow?"

"I'll be here."

She finished her salad. Hell, she'd wolfed the damn thing down. You got busy, you didn't have time to eat. Then you forgot to eat. Pretty soon you were starving. It was high time she had a shot and a Marlboro. She poured a double Cuervo neat and lit up and let the smoke slide down deep.

"Hey, Willie. Last call."

"Hmmmm?"

She watched the heavy eyelids slide up and then down again—what her father used to call the Long Blink. "Willie. Hey."

"Hmmmm?"

"Time to go."

"Oh yeah, 'course. Okay I finish this?" He smiled. "Sure."

She watched his fingers toy with the neck of the Heineken, literally feeling around for the thing, and then grip it and pour. He had about a third of a glass left. She took a hit of the Cuervo and another pull on the cigarette and walked around the service station and then down the bar past him to turn off the central air over by the plate-glass window and then heard the sounds of the city rush in to her left as the man opened the door and stepped through. The man nodded and smiled and took off his thin brown leather gloves and she thought, *shit, why does this always happen to me?* because she was supposed to stay open until one if there were any customers at all, that was the rule in this place and here it was twelve forty-five and it would be just her luck and she was just that new on the job that the boss would come around to check up on her if she told this guy she was closed already.

The man was tall and wore a good brown three-piece suit and he put his brown leather briefcase down on the bar eight stools back from Willie, just in front of the register and smiled again and said, *evening.*

"Evening," Willie said.

The man just looked at him.

She had to laugh.

"I'm just about to close," she said. So this'll be last call. But what can I get you?"

If he knew about anything he knew about bars and barflies and he could tell from the way the fat guy was sitting on his stool that he was about to drop, that she sure wasn't going to serve him again so that was when he'd made his move. He'd walked across the street from the flower shop where he'd been pretending to admire the window display and through the door. From where he stood he had a perfect view of the street and the corner of Columbus and 70th. Nice easy monitoring.

"What's on tap?" he said and she told him. He said he'd take the Amstel.

The Amstel came in a frosted mug. He liked that. He took a sip and watched her rinse a few glasses and dry her hands and then walk over to the fat guy in the corner. He liked the way she walked. It was assertive, very New York.

"Hey, Willie. Wake up, Willie."

"Huh?"

"Finish your beer."

"Right. Okay."

He tilted the glass and drank and set it down again.

"Tomorrow's another night, Willie. Finish it up."

"Okay." He did. "What I owe you?"

"You already paid me."

"I did?"

"Yep."

"Tip?"

"You left a good one, Willie. Thanks."

"Pleasure," he said and smiled and waved at her once like he was the goddamn Pope bestowing a drunk benediction and slid off the barstool. He tugged once at the collar of his faded gray raincoat and straightened up and managed not to stagger as he walked out the door.

God, he hated barflies. Fucking disgusting.

She went back to the dishes again.

"He's really a very nice guy," she said. "But with all that weight he's carrying I worry about him. I'm afraid he's going to have a heart attack or something right in the middle of my shift. Then what am I supposed to do?"

"I don't blame you. But say it did happen, what *would* you do?"

She shrugged. "Call 911 I guess. I've seen CPR but I've never, you know, actually done it."

"You've seen CPR?"

"Movies, television. Not in real life."

"Oh. I'm Larry by the way."

He put out his hand. She smiled and dried hers on a towel and took it.

"Claire. Nice to meet you."

"Nice to meet you, Claire."

He looked around while she went back to the glasses in the sink and thought, *hell, as good a time as any,* slipped on the surgical gloves out of her sightlines beneath the bar, unlatched the briefcase and opened it and pushed it aside with the top open so that it would block any view from the street and lay the gun down softly on the bar.

"Claire?"

She looked at him first and then at his hand spread over the gun and he watched her face change. He always liked this moment. *Revelation-time.*

"Here's what we're going to do, Claire. We're going to pretend we're a pair of old friends, maybe we even dated way back when, who knows? And I'm here closing up with you, so you do what you do every night, only I'm here. You lock the door and hit the lights outside and dim the ones in here. Only difference is that once you've done all that you empty the register into this briefcase. Me, I'm just having a drink. You understand?"

She nodded.

"Okay, now go on about your business. And Claire? Don't even think about trying to run out that door. I know you really want to very much right now but here's the thing, it takes too long to open the door, throw it back and then go through. Believe me, I know. You'll be dead before you hit the sidewalk. And I'm already up for Murder One in New York, New Jersey and Connecticut so it won't mean a thing to me one way or another."

He clicked off the safety.

"Do we have a meeting of the minds here, Claire?"

"Yes."

"Good. You know what you're supposed to do?"

"Yes."

"Then go."

"The keys are in my bag. The door keys."

"So? Get 'em."

He watched her, trying to gauge her reaction as she stooped down to the floor for her bag and set it in front of the speed rack and opened it and fished out her keyring. Her hands were shaking as she fumbled for the right one and that was good. Her color was off and that was good too.

But she kept glancing up at him—just before she stooped to retrieve her bag and then as she set it on the speed rack and then again as she turned the corner at the service station and a fourth time as she passed him headed for the door. He thought, *this one's a wiseass, she's trying to memorize what I look like,* but there were ways to minimize that possibility and ways to wipe it out almost completely.

It was called shock therapy.

The night had turned chilly and David was unprepared for that, dressed only in a light tan jacket and even with it zipped to the chin the wind off the river along West End Avenue was enough to send him immediately east all the way across to Central Park West where the packed-together rows of high-end residentials blocked it.

He walked from 63rd all the way up to 78th Street wondering what he was doing, keeping to the west side against the buildings both for the shelter and because you never knew about Central Park and who you might encounter this time of night. It was a lonely stretch though pretty well lit—a few people out walking their dogs or on their way home from somewhere or other and light two-way traffic. He supposed the street matched his mood. *Lonely and at least half-lit.*

At 78th he crossed three blocks over to Broadway though her bar was back on Columbus. He meant, he guessed, to describe a wide circle around her and only then, if he hadn't managed to shake this feeling by then, narrow in. He hoped the feeling would just go away. It was stupid, what he was doing. Even just standing across the street from the bar watching her through the plate-glass window would be stupid because if he could see her then there was also the possibility that she'd see him. Never mind that it was easily as humiliating as standing under her apartment window. To go inside and try to talk to her, which was what he really wanted to do, which was what he was aching to do, was bound to cause more hurt for both of them.

There could be no good ending to this.

But he was doing it anyway.

He headed down Broadway, hands shoved into his jeans against the cold. Some of the bars were still packed mostly with kids in their twenties and he heard music and loud laughter and other bars were still and dark, closed already or just about to close and the thought came to him suddenly that he had no idea how business was over at her place. She could easily have locked up and gone home by now. It was a definite possibility.

The thought filled him with a kind of dread and he picked up his pace so that by the time he crossed against the red and passed Grey Papaya at 72nd Street his heart was pounding so he slowed again. It wouldn't be good for her to see him this way, if he was going to be seen at all. He still wasn't sure about that. Wasn't sure what in the hell he was going to do.

But this feeling hadn't been mitigated being out here. The night air hadn't cleared his head or cured him. Not by a long shot. *He was so close.* To seeing her at least. To something.

He turned east at 70th and walked slowly toward Columbus.

She was going to keep this under control. He wouldn't use the gun.

He wanted the money, that's all.

Fine.

"I cashed out already," she said. "The money's in back."

"What's in the drawer?"

"Two hundred startup money for tomorrow."

"Put it in the briefcase. Cash box or safe?"

"Cash box, locked in the desk. They wouldn't trust me with the safe. I'm still new here."

"Oh? You're not trustworthy?"

"I'm new here."

She stacked the money in his briefcase. She watched him sip his beer.

"You already said that. But what I asked you is, are you trustworthy?"

"Y-yes."

Stop that, she thought. *Shit!* You don't want to show him fear. Not the slightest *bit* of fear.

"Should I trust you to go in back there and get the box for me?"

"Up to you."

He smiled and looked her up and down and she wished she'd worn something a little less clingy than the thin scoop-neck blouse.

"I don't think so," he said. "You're a woman. And I wouldn't trust a woman on a short leash with her fucking legs cut off. Nothing personal. Walk me back. And keep your hands down at your sides. Move."

She walked back through the tables and chairs stacked for the night back to the office and opened the office door and thought of slamming it in his face but that was only a thought and nothing she'd consider for a moment because all he wanted was the money. She found the right key for the drawer and opened it, took out the cash box and put it on the desk beside the printer and computer.

She turned.

And he was so close. The gun only inches from her chest. She lurched back and her hip hit the desk. It hurt. Her mouth was very dry all of a sudden.

"You want me to...I mean, should I open it? Or you want to just take it as it is?"

"Open it. I like to see what I've got."

He was smiling again and the brown eyes seemed to jitter back and forth and she thought strangely of ants or bees, of insects.

And there was no smile in the eyes at all.

It was a relief to turn back to the desk. Not to have to look at the eyes. She used three fingers against the box to steady her thumb and forefinger and finally found the keyhole and turned the key and turned and stepped away a little to her left. He lifted the lid.

"You had a good night, Claire."

He shut it again and took one step toward her, his face only inches from her face, directly in front of her.

"You really don't know CPR?"

"What?"

"You really don't know CPR? Just from what you see on television?"

"I never..."

"So what happens if some customer throws a fit or something? I'm just curious. Aren't you supposed to be *in charge* of this bar, Claire? Isn't that you? It's not the waiter who's in charge, it's not the fucking busboy. Is pouring a goddamn beer the only thing you're good for? What about responsibility? *Suppose I pitched a* fit *or something!* What would you do for me? Call 911 while I'm dying here? Jesus Christ!"

He's crazy, she thought. *He's a goddamn fucking lunatic and god knows what a lunatic will do.*

Maybe it isn't just the money.

And for the first time now he really scared her.

He had her now, he could tell by the look on her face, time to put the real fear of god into the bitch and see if she remembered anything *but* fear after that. He put the gun against her temple and backed her ass to the desk again.

"Open your mouth."

"What?"

"I said open your mouth. Do it, Claire."

She did.

"All right, now keep it open, understand? I'm gonna show you something. I'm gonna show you how to do CPR."

He reached over and pinched her nostrils shut. Her eyes skittered. He took a deep breath and put his mouth over hers and exhaled hard and heard her gasp when he pulled away and try to catch her breath but he did it again before she could, emptied his lungs into her and this time when he let her up for air she was coughing and her eyes were gleaming with tears.

She tasted like smoke and tequila.

The coughing stopped. She leaned back against the desk, chest heaving.

"There you go. Of course you'd be on your back, normally. But you get the idea. Grab the cash box. Come on."

He marched her back the way they'd come and saw her wipe her cheek with one hand and thought, *good start.*

David sat on the steps of a brownstone across the street from the ornate blue-and-gold Pythian building, a lit cigarette in his hand, trying to will his heart to stop pounding. He'd gotten halfway down the block when it felt like somebody had put a hand to his chest and said, *asshole, don't you take another step further.* Don't even think it.

He had no business being here.

Not on the steps, nobody would care about that—but being *here.* This close. Thinking what he was thinking.

She'd said she didn't want to see him, period and no hedging this time, that she couldn't see him, that seeing him had become a kind of grief played over and over again and that they simply had to stop, get away from one another and go lick their wounds until maybe in time they could be friends again or something like friends but that now they could be nothing.

It was the act of a willful selfish child to be this close to her.

What he needed to do was go home. Be an adult.

He'd made his choice. He should live with it.

He gasped at a sudden unexpected rush of tears. *That he should have to choose at all.* Not fair.

He wiped away the tears and drew on the cigarette and sat there, slowly calming.

"Pour me another Amstel, Claire. This one's gone flat. Use one of those good frozen mugs you've got there."

She did as he told her to do while he transferred the contents of the cash box to his briefcase, poured the beer and set it in front of him, trying to keep her hands from shaking, trying not to spill it, not to show. The taste of him was still in her mouth. He handed her the empty box.

"Put that on the floor or something, will you?"

She did that too, bent over and set it beside the garbage can and when she stood up again something hit her in the chest and she gasped, something freezing cold sliding down off her chest and over her belly.

He was laughing. The frosted glass was empty.

"Ooops. Little spill there. Gee, sorry."

"*You...!*"

He leaned in close over the bar.

"You *what*, Claire? You *what*? What do you want to call me? You want to call me names? Pour me another beer you dumb little shit and keep your fucking mouth shut. And I want a new glass."

She looked down at herself, arms out to her sides. She didn't know what to do. You could see almost everything through the thin material and the bra was thin too so you could even see her nipples puckered by the cold. *He* could see them, goddammit. If she brushed at it that would only make it worse, plastering the material to her body. She wanted to cry. *She wouldn't cry.* She turned to the freezer to get the glass and that was when she brushed herself off because then he couldn't see.

She drew the beer and set it in front of him on the bar. And almost wasn't surprised when he lifted it and threw it all over her again.

But when he laughed the second time, then she did cry. She couldn't help it. It just happened. Whether it was humiliation or frustration or fear or all of these together she just stood there, eyes closed and quietly sobbing.

"Look at me," he said.

She wouldn't. If she couldn't see him then she could almost pretend he couldn't see her.

"I said, look at me, dammit!"

She opened her eyes. What she saw was a man enjoying himself immensely. She couldn't understand. Why was he putting her through this? Shouldn't he be running away right now? Wasn't he at all worried about the cops?

How could anybody be like this?

"You stink of beer, Claire. Clean yourself off. You smell like a slut. Use that hand towel there. Dip it in some water. That's right. You have nice nipples, Claire. Say *thank you, sir*. I'm the customer. The customer's always right."

"Thank you."

She plucked the material out in front of her and wiped at it with the wet rag. The blouse was going to be stretched and ruined.

"Thank you, *sir*, Claire."

"Thank you, sir."

"Better. Now hand me that spindle."

"The what?"

"Jesus Christ, Claire, you've worked in bars for how long? The spindle. The goddamn spindle. The spike you stack your checks on, for chrissake!"

"I..."

She didn't want to do this. Her heart was suddenly hammering. She hated those things. Always had. Even just to look at them. The spike was maybe eight inches long rising straight up out of a thick coil of wire at its base. This one was set at the service station below one of the wine racks and whenever she had to climb up onto the counter to get to one of the more pricey wines up top she had visions of losing her balance and falling right onto it, of being impaled. She could see it. Ridiculous, horrible way to die.

The spike was as sharp and thick as an icepick.

"Please...I don't..."

"Ah, begging. I like that."

"Those things scare me, okay?"

"Why? You use it every day."

"They just do."

"Maybe I want to scare you."

"What? Please..."

"Maybe I want to scare you. Maybe I don't like you one goddamn bit, Claire, and maybe I want to scare you so much I could almost come in my pants just thinking about it? What if the money's only a kind of perk? Maybe this is what it's all about. You ever consider that, you dopey whore?"

"Why...?"

"*Why?* Because I want to. Because this gun tells us both I can. You hear me, you ugly fuck? You get ugly when you cry, Claire, you know that? *You want to know why? Because after me you'll never feel safe again, Claire. Never. Not at work, not at home. Nowhere. Because that's my wish for the whole fucking world and for you, Claire, in particular.* Now hand me the goddamn spindle!"

She could barely see him through the tears but she could feel the heat of his anger reach out to her across the bar. For a split second she imagined him bursting into flame. *Where did all this come from? Why? What had she done?*

David thought, *if she hates me for it, so be it. I have to see her.*

He crushed out the cigarette and stepped down off the brownstone.

"I want to show you how we're gonna do this, Claire. Stop blubbering for chrissake. Take one of those cocktail napkins there. Wipe your goddamn nose. You're gonna do it once first, just so you can see how hard it is, and then it's my turn. See, I put my hand on the bar, palm down, just like this. Then you pick up the spindle. You raise it over the center of my hand to exactly the level of this beer mug, no lower and no higher. Lower's cheating. Higher and it'll never work. Then you try to spike me."

"I can't..."

"Sure you can. I'll give you some incentive. You spike me and the game's over right now and you get to keep whatever's in your tip jar. I don't think you will, though. Like I say, it's hard. Assuming you don't, then I get three tries. I miss all three, you keep whatever's in your tip jar. I don't miss...well, then you're shit out of luck, Claire. Now pick up the spindle. And remember, the gun's in the other hand so you don't want to be thinking about doing anything else with it other than playing our little game."

He watched her eyes. The eyes always flickered when they made their move. The eyes were a dead giveaway. But he didn't even need the eyes this time. Instead of bringing it straight on down she raised it a half inch first so it was an easy thing to pull his hand away. Gave it a lot of force, though. She was game, he gave her that much. He freed the spindle from the bar.

"Okay. My turn."

"No. Please. Just take the money. Just leave me alone, please? Enough, all right? All right??"

The husky voice had turned into a whine. The eyes were red with tears.

He smiled.

"Not enough, Claire. Not all right. But what are you worried about? You saw how tough it is. I'll probably lose anyway, right? Of course maybe I won't."

"I can't, please..."

"You can, Claire. You have to. See the gun? See this tubing at the end? It's called a silencer. I made it myself. That means I can shoot you three or four times if I want to without even killing you, you dumb piece of shit and nobody's going to hear it, the neighbors upstairs will never be the wiser. And *that*, Claire, is a world of pain, I promise you. You want it to go down that way? Fine by me. Different game is all. Nastier."

"Oh, jesus! Why...?"

"You know the little *pffttt* sound silencers always make in the movies? Doesn't happen. More like car door closing. So what'll it be?"

She thought of her widowed mother in Queens and how in another month it would be Christmas and then of her sister married three months almost to the day and pregnant out in Oregon and that she'd never visited, thought of the paintings just finished and half-finished and of David still not free of her nor her of him and she thought about the kitten who curled between her feet each night and who would feed her and take care of her and apprehended something of what the world would be like without her in it, an almost impossible concept just an hour ago but glimpsed now for a moment and thought *I'm so afraid, I'm so afraid of what I won't get to see and she put her hand down on the bar.*

...and now his control is complete. He can see it in her eyes. He can see she knows a truth he's known all along, that there is no help in this world, that

what will happen will happen and no amount of pleading to god or jesus or to the milk of human kindness will get you any goddamn where at all, that in the face of loathing as deep and strong as his is she is just another worker ant in an anthill he can bring down in a second, crush beneath his feet at any time he wishes—her hand on the bar says all of this to him, and the temptation is there to do it to her on the very first plunge of the spike, to bring it instantly into even more stark perspective for her, the perspective of flesh, of spilled blood, of pain.

Yet he resists that. He lets her pull away and listens to her gasp and the dull thud of the spindle against the bar and raises it again and watches her hand slide across the bar to submit a second time and wonders, is she hopeful? Does she see an end to this? Because he seems to have missed? That this might be true is delightful to him too because he can wipe it all away so quickly, he has lied again and he is very good at this, he has had practice and if hope is not yet there he can place it in her heart on this second try, bait his trap for the hungry animal which is all she is after all— hungry for the truth of what he knows to be.

And this time he can practically hear her heart beating, racing as she pulls away because yes! He can feel the hope there coiled in her like a snake—he has missed by a mile it seems to her and he can smell the stink of hope, its sudden sweet reek as he positions the spike above her hand a third and final time and then, prescient and sly and born of months and years watching his back, trusting his senses, he glances out the plate-glass window to the street...

"Who the hell is that?" he says.

And at first she can only think it's part of this game he's playing, this insane evil fucked-up game and she doesn't look up at all but only at her hand on the bar waiting for the courage to pull it away if she can a third time but then the words and the tone of the words seem to spill through to her and what she hears is unexpected, wrong in these circumstances, a flat even tone as if he'd said *well that's interesting, it's raining out* and she looks first at him and then at where he's looking and sees David on the corner by the closed dark flower shop across the street. Their eyes meet and he's scowling, puzzled and she thinks, *oh no, oh god no, I was so close, I might have finished this here and now.* She remembers seeing him down on the street across from her apartment building many nights ago and drawing away from the curtain before he glimpsed her at the window and remembers thinking how terribly sad it was for both of them and how wasteful that she could never, ever have come out to meet him and thinks *David, why in hell are you here again? What in hell have you done now?*

She holds his gaze and slowly shakes her head. Don't even think it. The scowl disappears. Instead the eyes plead with her, confused and uncertain. Eyes so well known and loved. She needs to deny these eyes. For both of them.

"Who is he, Claire?"

"My...boyfriend. Ex-boyfriend."

"Ex?"

"We've broken up."

"So what's he doing here?"

"I don't know."

The man seems to think a moment.

She watches David take a step closer to the curb. She shakes her head again. *No, goddammit!* Don't *do* this! *Please,* you fucking lovely idiot, stay the hell *away!*

"I think you'd better invite him in, Claire."

"No."

"Oh yes. You have to."

"I won't."

"Yes you will. Or it's you first and then him. Twenty seconds is all I need. He'll never know what hit him."

He closes the briefcase beside him and snaps it shut and slides the spindle down the bar well beyond her reach.

He's ready to go now. The game is over. All of it over now unless she brings David into this and if she does, won't it just begin again? To what end? Why does he want this?

What can he hope to gain? He can walk out the door right now. Free and clear. Just walk away.

Her eyes go back to David. To hold him there. *Don't move.*

"Do it."

"I can't."

"You will."

She thinks—hard and fast as best she can. *She will not do this to him.* And there seems only one way to do that. To convince him that she's furious at him for being there. He ought to be able to believe that. He ought to have anticipated that reaction from her. She has every right to be furious—though she's not. Though seeing him again even under these terrible circumstances feels so tender that what she'd like to do is embrace him, hug him, sob into his shoulder not just for what this man has put her through tonight but for all they've lost and all they had. To do that one more time again. What she'd sworn she'd never do.

She moves out past the service station and turns and heads past the man to the door.

Outside on the corner David sees her long purposeful familiar stride but the look on her face is unfamiliar. It's a look he can't quite read. When he'd thought he knew them all. He's only just arrived here but already something feels wrong about her and he thinks, who's this guy in there? New boyfriend? Boss? But boyfriend doesn't feel right. Of course it's possible he just doesn't want to admit that she might already have one. Might already have replaced him.

But boyfriend doesn't feel right. Nor does boss. Something about her face, the look in her eyes.

A car passes and then another. Claire is at the lock now.

He steps out into the street.

Claire looks up from the lock and he's crossing, coming toward her and she feels the blood rush to her face, pulse pounding and she flings open the door *because she will not expose him to this goddammit, she will not permit that* and summons the most dismissive angry tone of which she is capable and shouts out into the still night air.

"DAVID! GO! GET..."

...OUT OF HERE! is what she means to say...

...but the sheer sudden size of her voice startles the man inside and he thinks...HELP! THE POLICE! *she's calling for help the stupid bitch* so he turns and fires and the flower blooms wet in her back and he hears the silencer like a door closing exactly as he's told her it would be and she falls spilled to one side, the glass door wedged open by her hips and he pulls the briefcase off the bar thinking *the fucking cop was right, he's finally had to shoot somebody* and the boyfriend is almost across the street closing the gap between them and as he steps over her body he sees her eyes flutter stunned and wide and the man is yelling *Claire! Claire!* loud enough to wake the dead, the man not exactly understanding yet he thinks but there's no way to know what he'll do once he does so as he turns a sharp right headed toward the subway at 72nd he fires again and watches, for a just a moment, a second flower bloom across the man's chest, watches him sink to his knees and fall and reach for her, the man's hand settling in her flung tangled hair along the sidewalk, his hand opening and closing in strands of hair, unable to reach further.

He doesn't know if he feels fear. He might. Maybe he should.

But he knows he feels good.

David lies sprawled along the sidewalk. The sidewalk feels oddly warm to him. It ought to feel cold this time of year. He tries to move but can't. He tries to breathe and barely can. Is this shock? Death? What? He sees her lying near him in the doorway. If he focuses on her, on Claire, he might live, someone might come by.

That he might even want to live disgusts him.

She stares up, blinks into empty sky.

Tears again.

So many tears in this city. So much heartbreak.

Then none.

Thanks to Amy, Mila, and Adonis.

I apologize for feeling I had to leave you with this one.

For months after 9/11 I wasn't able write at all. Fiction seemed utterly trivial to me. Particularly fictional terrors. I had a conversation with Peter Straub at our local waterhole one evening and he confessed to having the same problem. As New Yorkers each of us found it wholly understandable.

But writing's what we do.

So eventually it occurred to me that one way to solve my problem was to write about terror directly—though on a smaller canvas—with the World Trade Center as backdrop but with personal *mano-a-mano* terrorism front and center. Metaphor as story-line.

What I wrote turned out to be the most bleak and hopeless piece I'd ever produced. And it was only after I read the galleys for the Leisure paperback edition of *Peacable Kingdom*—in which the story first appeared—that I realized exactly why.

I hadn't really written about terror at all.

I'd written about loss.

Irreversible, irretrievable loss.

Pas sto kalo.
It's Greek to me.
Go with the good.

Jack Ketchum

About the Author

Jack Ketchum's first novel, *Off Season*, prompted the *Village Voice* to publicly scold its publisher in print for publishing violent pornography. He personally disagrees but is perfectly happy to let you decide for yourself. His short story "The Box" won a 1994 Bram Stoker Award from the HWA, his story "Gone" won again in 2000—and in 2003 he won Stokers for both best collection for *Peaceable Kingdom* and best long fiction for *Closing Time*. He has written twelve novels, arguably thirteen, five of which have been filmed – *The Girl Next Door*, *Red*, *The Lost*, *Offspring* and *The Woman*, written with Lucky McKee. His stories are collected in *The Exit at Toledo Blade Boulevard*, *Peaceable Kingdom*, *Closing Time and Other Stories*, and *Sleep Disorder*, with Edward Lee. His horror-western novella *The Crossings* was cited by Stephen King in his speech at the 2003 National Book Awards. He was elected Grand Master for the 2011 World Horror Convention.

Curious about other Crossroad Press books?
Stop by our website:
www.crossroadpress.com
or visit our online store at:
http://store.crossroadpress.com
We offer quality writing
in digital, audio, and print formats.

Enter the code FIRSTBOOK
to get 20% off your first order from our store!
Stop by today!

Printed in Great Britain
by Amazon

85690449R00120